AF147253

Evil Eye In The Western Highlands

By

R. C. Maclagan

Double 9
BOOKS

Evil Eye In The Western Highlands
by R. C. Maclagan

Copyright © 2024

All Rights reserved.

No part of this publication may be reproduced,
stored in a retrieval system, or transmitted in any
form or by any means, electronic, mechanical,
photocopying or Otherwise, without the written
permission of the publisher.
The author/editor asserts the moral right to
be identified as the author/editor of this work.

ISBN: 978-93-61423-15-4

Published by

DOUBLE 9 BOOKS

2/13-B, Ansari Road
Daryaganj, New Delhi – 110002
info@double9books.com
www.double9books.com
Tel. 011-40042856

This book is under public domain

ABOUT THE AUTHOR

R. C. Maclagan, a.k.a. Rachel Harriette Busk was a writer, translator, and folklorist from Britain. She was born into a Scottish-English household in London, England. Maclagan received his education at home and from an early age showed a strong interest in mythology, folklore, and languages. Because of her love of folklore, Maclagan emerged in the late 19th century as one of the leading authorities on British folklore studies. She gathered and recorded a great deal of myths, folklore, and folktales from all across the British Isles, including Scotland, Wales, and Ireland. Maclagan's book "Evil Eye in the Western Highlands," which examines the cultural practices and beliefs surrounding the evil eye phenomena in the Scottish Highlands, is one of her most significant contributions to folklore studies. Throughout her career, Maclagan made a substantial contribution to the preservation and propagation of old folk beliefs and practices, which in turn enhanced the general public's comprehension of British folklore and cultural heritage. Even now, academics and fans of folklore studies still regard her work highly.

CONTENTS

INTRODUCTION 9

EVIL EYE 15

LOCALITY OF BELIEF 21

SOCIAL POSITION OF BELIEVERS 22

DESCRIPTION OF POSSESSORS OF EVIL EYE 24

OBJECTION TO MEETING AN EVIL EYE 27

AVOIDING SUSPICION OF EVIL EYE 29

ACTION OF EVIL EYE
INDEPENDENT OF POSSESSOR 31

EVIL EYE TAKES EFFECT EVEN
ON THINGS NOT SEEN 33

MORAL SOURCE OF THE EVIL EYE 35

THINGS THAT SPECIALLY ATTRACT 37

STRANGERS SPECIALLY LIABLE TO BE
ACCUSED OF THE POSSESSION OF THE EVIL EYE 39

PEOPLE SHOULD GIVE WHEN ASKED 41

SYMPTOMS IN ANIMALS ASCRIBED
TO EFFECT OF EVIL EYE 43

BENEFIT TO THE OWNER OF AN EVIL EYE 53

DISADVANTAGE TO THE OWNER
OF AN EVIL EYE 55

CONSEQUENCE OF DIRECT PRAISE 59

A LOOK DOES IT 62

AVOIDING THE LOOK 65

CONVERSION TO BELIEF IN EVIL EYE............68

GIVING AWAY MILK DANGEROUS............69

SCIENCE VERSUS EOLAS............70

HURTER AND HEALER............75

TRANSMISSION OF EOLAS............77

FORMS OF INCANTATION............79

FORM OF PAYMENT............81

THE NECESSITY OF FAITH............84

PREVENTING EVIL BY BLESSING............85

PREVENTING BY DISPRAISING............87

PREVENTING BY ROWAN AND JUNIPER............88

PREVENTING BY HORSE NAILS AND SHOES............90

PREVENTING BY A SMALL GIFT............91

A PREVENTATIVE BY BURNING CLOTHING............93

PREVENTION BY SPITTING............94

PREVENTING BY CHURNING............96

PREVENTION BY PECULIARITY IN CLOTHES............98

TAR AS PREVENTATIVE............99

NICKING THE EAR............100

URINE AS PREVENTATIVE............101

A BURNT OFFERING............104

CHARMS. (STRING)............105

UISGE A' CHRONACHAIDH (WATER OF INJURY)............111

STONES AND WATER............121

IRON AND WATER............124

WOOD AND WATER............126

SALT AS CURE AND PREVENTATIVE 127

MOST SUITABLE WATER 130

TABOO WHEN IN POSSESSION OF WATER 132

WATER, WHERE APPLIED 137

ODD CURES 139

AN EYE FOR AN EYE...142

SHOWING WHO IS THE MISCHIEF MAKER 145

PUTTING ELSEWHERE 151

APPENDIX...154

INDEX...158

INTRODUCTION

The Evil Eye is a superstition arising not from local circumstances, or peculiarity of a great or small division of the human family, but is a result of an original tendency of the human mind. The natural irritation felt at the hostile look of a neighbour, still more of an enemy, is implanted in the breast of all, however much they may be influenced by moral teaching. When we add to this the feeling that some valued possession has attracted the coveteous desire of another, the fear of loss is added to the irritation of mere anger. To some such natural feeling we must ascribe the belief in an Evil Eye.

Theories of an origin more restricted, founded on the fear of loss or damage to particular possessions of individuals guaranteed them by the custom of law, developed in the community of which they form part, scarcely satisfy after inquiry. Where a subsistence can be easily procured the Evil Eye would be little regarded in connection with food, but might naturally develop itself in connection with the relations of the sexes. No doubt the latter, the most interesting to individuals of all passions, causes feelings of hostility between rivals universally, but where the food supply is difficult to procure one would naturally expect that damage from the covetous desires of others, where they seemed to affect the life-preserving store, would become equally important.

In the following study of the belief of an Evil Eye among the Gaelic-speaking peoples of Scotland at the present day, an attempt is made neither to disguise nor to improve upon what those in contact with believers have learned from their mouths. The writer is a believer in the Evil Eye only in so far as it may be a term for the natural selfishness of the human being, as a "tender heart" is a recognised way of speaking of a nature apt to sympathy. Selfishness, natural to all of us, is apt to find expression in our habits, however much we may disguise it by religious or charitable profession. Were it a part of our nature to have for our neighbour the same affection that we have for ourselves, no such superstition as that of the Evil Eye could have arisen. But we are not made that way, and so reformers, in endeavouring to cure this sin, as they consider it, have preached and tried to practise such ordinances as "Thou shalt not covet," and "Thou shalt love thy neighbour as thyself." Truly hard sayings, and in nine hundred and ninety-nine cases out of a thousand with difficulty getting beyond the status of a pious opinion.

Not that that teaching has been without effect; and we may hope that with the extension of communications and the progress gradually being made to that condition of things where

"Man to man the world o'er

Shall brithers be for a' that,"

the *bad e'e* may some day in these isles be merely a study for folklorists as Totemism is, and as difficult to find as an auk's egg.

Right or wrong, the theory here advanced accounts, satisfactorily, as far as the writer can judge, for the present-day widespread belief in Scotland of the power for evil of the glance of the human eye.

As will be seen afterwards, there are those who theorise on the bad heart influencing the eye, the ill effect of the Evil Eye only arising from the glance of the covetous; but this is probably the result of preconceived religious ideas, and of the moral teaching to which its believers have been accustomed. It is not to be wondered at; it would be impossible indeed, but that the teaching of Christianity should have affected and given a direction to this ancient superstition. Thus we find it Christianised to a marked degree, its origin is conceived of as a breaking of the commandment "Thou shalt not covet," and its cures are mostly connected with a reference to the Deity, and to the Trinity of the Christian. The magic thread with the three knots on it, though heathen in its origin, has surely some connection with the rosary, the aspersion with water, with baptism, and the holy water of the Roman Church. But it is not a superstition introduced with Christianity, it is as native as the heather of our hills, or the sandstone rock of the Coronation Stone.

This statement might be safely enough advanced upon general principles, but we are not without satisfactory literary evidence of what we advance. In the Ossianic *"Acallam na Senorach"* (The Colloquy with the Ancient Men), the second longest prose composition of the mediæval Irish, a collection (probably made in the late twelfth or thirteenth century) of separate stories united together in one framework, we find the following as related in MSS. of the fifteenth century and later.

The Fiann are on a visit to the King of Munster. The son of the King of Ulster marries the daughter of the King of Munster.

"The damsel bore him a famous and beautiful son named Fer Oc ('young man'), and in all Ireland there were scarcely one whose shape and vigour and spear-casting were as good as his."

On a subsequent visit, the three battalions of the Fiann are lost in admiration of the activity and skill of a young man who turns out to be this Fer Oc. "Then was a hunt and a battue held by the three battalions of the Fiann. Howbeit, on that day, owing to Fer Oc (and his superior skill) to none of the Fiann it fell to get first blood of pig or deer. Now when they came home, after finishing the hunt, a sore lung-disease attacked Fer Oc, through the (evil) eyes of the multitude and the envy of the great host, and it killed him, soulless, at the end of nine days." "He was buried on yonder green-grassed hill," says Cailte, "and the shining stone that he held when he was at games and diversion is that yonder rising out of his head." [1] The Gaelic here simply says "*tre tsuilib na sochaide*" (through the eyes of the multitude), and it will be seen that modern reciters sometimes speak in exactly the same way of the "eye" unqualified, but meaning the Evil Eye. But there is more than this in the story; it is a young man who suffers, and the young are most easily affected. It is a remarkable and handsome youth that suffers, and what attracts the eye, especially beauty, is peculiarly liable to injury, and the statement is made that it was the envious glance which affected the victim. *Cormac's Glossary* (an Irish compilation begun in the tenth century, and added to throughout the Middle Ages), preserved in MSS. of the commencement of the fifteenth century, mentions the Evil Eye:—

> *Milled* (spoiling, hurting, (b) *i.e. mi shilledh*, a mislook, *i.e.* an evil eye).
>
> *Millead i mi shillead i silled olc.* [Or as in another MS.]
>
> *Milliud quasi mishilliud i drochshilliud.*

To this O'Clery adds "*no droch amharc*," while O'Donovan's note at (b) is "the evil eye," "the injury done by the evil eye." [2]

[1] *Irische Texte.* Stokes and Windisch, fourth series, vol i. pp. 232, 234, 161.

[2] *Cormac's Glossary*, translated by O'Donovan, edited by Whitley Stokes, p. 107; and *Three Irish Glossaries*, by W. S., p. 28.

Our business is with the so-called facts of the Evil Eye, and whether or not in this case the philology of the compiler of the *Glossary* is right, there can be no sort of doubt of the allusion being to the present living belief in the Evil Eye.

Apart from the doing of evil, and causing sickness and death without immediate increase to the possessions of the witch, the effect of the Evil Eye centres round the natural covetousness of the greedy person. Where the owner of an evil eye gets no benefit himself, the effect ascribed is always to diminish what he might envy in the possession of another. It is always the young and *toradh* of cattle (milk and butter), or the fruits of the labour of the owner that is lessened or destroyed. Whatever the philological root of this word *toradh*, it must surely be allied with the irregular verb *thoir* (give); and though there seems at first sight no close relationship between personal beauty and a good churning, yet both of them are highly prized gifts. *Toradh* means fruit produce; thus Cain's offering was the *toradh* of the earth.

The expression used in Kintyre for the power of taking away produce is *pisreag*. In Arran the word applied to the curative measures is *pisearachd*. *Piseach* means increase; thus in Proverbs xviii. 20, where it is said that a man shall be filled with the "increase of his lips," the Gaelic word used is *piseach*, and so it comes to mean progeny and good fortune. *Piseach ort* (Good fortune be yours). Irish Gaelic gives *piseog* (witchcraft). Surely this is a secondary meaning from the idea of increase and good fortune being in certain cases brought about by charms and witchery. And thus we have found *pisearachd* explained as the Arran and Kintyre equivalent for *geasarachd*, of which all the evidence seems to favour its primary signification being connected with spells and charms.

Another word which has been used to collectors for *eolas* (science of its own magical sort) is *fiosachd*, which the dictionaries give as meaning "foretelling," "augury." This seems to be a secondary and limited application of a term meaning possession of *fios* (knowledge, information).

The popular mixing up of legitimate curative measures, such as come from the administration of drugs, with what undoubtedly is considered illegitimate, namely, the use of charms and sorcery in general, is of course as common as can be in the experience of those in contact with genuine savagery, but it occurs also nearer home. A native of Arran tells how she remembers an old woman, of whom the people were afraid because she was supposed to be a witch. The groundwork of this accusation was that she was to be often seen gathering herbs, and the reciter remembers when she herself was a girl, that, to use her own words, it was "the fright of her life" to meet her in a lonely place, or in the dark.

An inquiry such as this has to be conducted with care. The believer is sensitive to ridicule, and would take as a mortal offence being publicly gibbeted, so as to cause animadversion from others, even when he himself is convinced of the truth of his beliefs and sayings. For this reason we must be excused giving the name and residence of the various reciters.

The information has to be drawn in general conversation and incidentally, but every care has been taken to avoid recounting anything in which *mala fides* is suspected. We consider in many cases things told by a daughter of her mother, or a son of his father, as equally reliable as if detailed by himself when we know they have been recited originally for information of the juniors. Undoubtedly the younger generation are in many cases more critical than their forefathers; but we have no hesitation in maintaining that what will hereafter be set down allows of a fairly perfect appreciation of the belief of the great majority of the less educated class, and of many much above that in the West Highlands, up to the introduction of the School Board as a universal institution. Of course there always were doubters, and the tricks played to take a rise out of a believer by an unbeliever may sometimes figure as accepted evidence of the bad effects of the Evil Eye, when it was a trick played off merely for fun, though in other cases deliberately intended to mislead. Tricks, however, will not carry us back to an original cause, however much they may have helped the maintenance of the belief in superstitious minds. These fail entirely in power of appreciation of the jocular, when what is done is dangerous according to their ideas. A strong believer in the Evil Eye, and of course much afraid of it, in the island of Skye, was one day out among the cows. Two of his neighbours passing, one of them, a bit of a wag, said to his companion: "*Bheir mi da sgillinn duit ma theid thu agus do cheann a chuir fodh'n mhart sin agus glaodh 'nach mor an t-uth tha aig a bho*" ("I will give you twopence if you will go and put your head under that cow and cry, Hasn't the cow the big udder?")

The fellow agreed, and went and bent his head under the cow and shouted out at the top of his voice, calling Rory's attention to his supposititious admiration of the remarkable development of the cow in question. The man tempted to make the remark was "a little soft." Rory at once thinking of the Evil Eye, seized his stick and rushed at him, threatening to break his head if he would not at once bless the cow. The suborned perpetrator of the joke, it need scarcely be said, at once took the method demanded to counteract his injudicious praise. How many of us are, not in the belief of the Evil Eye, but in other beliefs, just as touchy as our friend Rory.

The stick may be good enough for a defence of superstition, but ridicule is the proper method of attack.

A young intelligent lady was lately in a house in the village of Golspie, the occupant of which, mourning over the dying of her fowls, said she suspected it was the result of the Evil Eye of Mrs. X., a neighbour. The next day, being in the same house, another neighbour came in carrying a growing plant, which she presented to the complainer, saying: "Mrs. X. told me that you had your eye on this, and ever since it has done no good; the leaves have been withering and falling off. Now!—there it is to you! keep it."

The person superstitious enough to believe in the force of the Evil Eye may well be expected to have his superstitious faculty developed in other directions. A child took ill, and its parents believed it was the Evil Eye of a certain woman which had done the harm. With the view of bringing her to confess her doings, or in any case to punish her, they procured a square of turf, and having stuck a lot of pins in it, they placed it on the fire. This action, one of the forms of the so-called *corp creadha*, was intended to do personal injury to the suspected party. There was no evidence of it having had any effect whatever.

EVIL EYE

After the long existence in this country of Christianity, while we talk composedly of the superstitions of the heathen and of other Christian nations, we are apt to forget our own, or if we speak of them, we look on them pityingly as peculiar to some individuals of whose opinion we reckon little. In towns, and among those who read many books, the constant friction of man against man hinders the survival of a belief in such a thing as the Evil Eye, now that a certain quantity of education is common property. Where the incidents of life are less crowded, and individual experiences are rarer and at longer intervals, that is, in country districts and especially in the more mountainous and less closely populated, the Evil Eye has yet in Scotland many believers, and consequently considerable influence. Such a remark as the following, made to a minister, is not so rare as one might suppose: "Nae doot whatever Mac had the Evil Eye, that's certain. I have known many cases when a calf, or even a cow, died the day after he looked at her." Another said of the same: "I was once in the dairy when he came in. 'You should not have let that bad man in,' said Nancy MacIntyre to me. 'Why?' said I. 'Because he has an Evil Eye,' said she. Now, I will not say that this was true, but this I know, that on that very day one of the cows bursted, and died from eating clover. What do ye say to that?"

Another sample is the following: A farmer's son, whose father had lost a horse, was thus addressed by a neighbour, "You had a horse that was ill, is it better?" "Oh no, it is dead." "You are unfortunate this year. Isn't that four that have died on you?" "Yes, but we know now what was wrong with them." "Weel, that's well; ye'll know what to do should any more take ill. What was wrong with them?" "They were *air-an-cronachadh*" (harmed). "Such nonsense! there is nothing of that now." The lad did not agree with this, said they knew who did it, and the lad's interrogator's mother-in-law joined in the conversation, agreeing as to the correctness of the diagnosis; and the doubter rejoined, "Well, if you are all against me, I may stop."

An Argyllshire islander says:—

"*Tha buideachas uile air falbh anis agus is math gu bheil, oir be ni olc a bha ann. Ach, ma dh'fhalbh sin, tha rud eile nach d'fhalbh fathast, agus 'se sin cronachadh. Chunnaic m'i ann mo thigh fein mucuircean, agus thainig ban-choimhearsnach a steach latha, agus thubhairt i gum bu mhuc ciatach a bha'n sin. 'Tha i gle mhath,' fhreagair mi fhein. Well, chaidh am boireannach a mach, agus cha robh i tiota air falbh, nur a thug a mhuc an aon sgreach aisde agus air dol mun cuairt dith, thuit i air an urlar. Le so, thainig D. 'ac A. a stigh, agus fheoraich e 'Co an t-aon mu dheireadh a chunnaic a mhuc?' Dh' innis mi fhein dha, gum be a leithid so 'a bhean. 'Mata' ars esan, 's ise rinn an t-olc. Ach ma tha uillidh sam bi lar ruit, cha chreid mi gum bi mise fada ga cuir ceirt. Fhuair mi dha uillidh nam piocach, agus ghabh e a mhuc eadar a dha chois, agus thaom e lan copa dheth na beul. Thug a mhuc reibhig, agus shaoil mi fhein gu robh i air chuthach ach ann a' mionaid a dh'uine, bha i ceirt gu leoir; Nis, nach be sud an droch bhean?"*

("Witchcraft is all gone now, and it is well it is, for it was a bad thing. But if that is gone, there is another thing that has not gone yet, and that is *Cronachadh*. I saw a breeding sow in my own house, and one day a neighbour came in, and she said that that was a splendid sow. I answered that she was very good. Well, the woman went out, and she was no time away when the sow gave such a scream, and going round about she fell on the floor. With this D. Mac A. came in, and he asked who was the last person that had seen the sow. I told him it was such and such a woman. 'Well,' said he, 'it was she that did the harm, but if you have any oil beside you, I believe I shall not be long putting her right.' I got saithe oil for him, and he took the sow between his two legs, and poured a cupful into her mouth. She screamed, and I thought she was mad, but in a minute's time she was all right. Now, wasn't that the bad woman?")

A young fellow who had received a liberal education, in fact, a probationer of the Church, the son of a self-made man, fairly well-to-do, avowed his own belief in the Evil Eye. He said in effect: "As sure as you and I are sitting here there is an Evil Eye in it. I know that when I was in Harris, and our M. an infant, there was a certain woman who used to come in pretty often, the sister-in-law of H., you know, and my wife, who you know is not one to tell a lie or speak about these things, told me that every time that woman came in she would be praising the child, and the child was always unwell after it."

We thus see, though we know that ministers of the Church are by their profession kept in the dark on matters of which they would express unbelief, yet that where a superstition is ingrained in a parishioner it is not concealed from the minister. Ministers may be misled by putting their own interpretation on the form in which the information comes to them. A clergyman in one of the Western Islands said: "I have observed that there is still a strong belief in blighting from the Evil Eye among the people in the parish of K. A respectable and intelligent man whom I visited often during a season of sickness, once and again, when talking about his illness, made the remark '*fhuair mi cronachadh*.' I always misunderstood what the man meant by *cronachadh*, taking it in the sense of reproof, and therefore thinking that what was meant was that the sufferer was placed under chastisement by a dispensation of Providence. At last, however, I learned from a third person that the sick man was strongly impressed with the belief that his illness was caused by some evil-intentioned person who had wished him ill." This suggests witchcraft as much as or even more than the Evil Eye; but the two things run into each other more or less. We have already seen one Gaelic reciter maintaining that witchcraft, *buidseachas*, did not now exist, but the Evil Eye did. Compare that with this from a native of Uist:—

"*Ma ta bha buidseashas ann. Chaidh mi fhein aon latha gu tigh coimhearsnaich airson coileach oig, agus bha laogh aca ceangailte aig cul an doruis. Cha robh mi fada san tigh gus an d'thainig nighean a steach. 'Nuair a fhuair mise an t-eun, dh'fhalbh mi, agus cha robh mi ach beagan uine air falbh 'nuair a dh'fhas an laogh tinn. Chuir muinntir an tighe fios thun boireannach a bha 'n sin, aig an robh sgil mu bhuidseachas, mar bhiodh daoine 'g radh, ga h-iarruidh a thighinn a dh'-amhairc an laogh. Thainig am boireannach, ach ma thainig, bha an laogh marbh mus d'thainig i. Co luath 's a dh'amhairc i air thubhairt i riutha air an spot gum b'e 'n "suill" a dh'aobhraich am bas. Agus air bharrachd air sin, dh'innis i dhoibh co rinn an gonadh. So mar thubhairt i. "Nach robh dithist bhoireannaich agaibh an so am eigin an diugh?" Agus 'nuair a fhreagair iad gun robh, thubhairt ise. "Bha h-aon diubh soilleir, agus an te eile dorcha. Bha shawl glas air an te shoilleir, agus b'bise a dh'oibrich am buidseachas.*"

"*Nis bha sin gle fhior, oir bha an nighean a thainig a steach nur bha mise san tigh soilleir, agus bha shawl glas oirre cuideachd.*"

"Indeed, witchery was in it. I myself went one day to a neighbour's house for a young cock, and they had a calf tied behind the door. I was not long in the house till a girl came in. When I got the bird I went away, and I was only a short time away when the calf became unwell. The people of the house sent word to a woman that was there, who had skill of witchery, as people would be saying, asking her to come to look at the calf. The woman came, but if (she) came, the calf was dead before she came. As soon as she looked on it, she said to them on the spot, that it was the 'Eye' that caused the death. And more than that, she told them who had done the mischief (wounding). Here is how she said: 'Have you not had two women here sometime to-day?' and when they answered that there had been, she said: 'One of them was fair and the other dark. There was a grey shawl on the fair one, and it was she that wrought the witchery.' Now that was quite true, for the girl that came in when I was in the house was fair, and there was a grey shawl on her."

A woman of about sixty-five, a reader of history and Gaelic publications, remembers when the belief in the Evil Eye was so common in Islay, that when any disease came among a person's cattle, it gave rise at once to a strong suspicion that they had been *air an cronachadh*. The disease was called "*dosgach*." When one would come with the news of disease or death among a neighbour's cattle, the person to whom it was told would say, "*Mach an dosgach a so*"; or, "*Mach a so an droch sgeul*" ("Away the plague from here;" or, "Away the evil news from here.") At the same time, suiting the action to the words, he would tear some piece off the clothes he had on at the time and throw it into the fire. This was supposed to prevent the evil from coming his way.

Indeed there are very many who still act on the belief expressed in the following, by an old distillery workman, uneducated, but naturally shrewd, though we would say credulous: "They will be saying to me that we have no mention of *cronachadh* in the Bible, and they will be putting it down my throat, but I tell them that it is there. Both the Evil Eye and Witchcraft were in it from the beginning, and they will be in it till the end."

We may mention here that there is a very strong belief among many of the influence of the "wish" for good or evil. "B. McL. affirms that if she wishes ill to any person ill is sure to follow, and if she wishes well good will come of it. She maintained that a person, lately dangerously ill, owed her recovery to her good wishes." A person has only to maintain this view, and the superstitious will probably find reasons for believing that it is true. This, however, opens the question of the *guidhe* (imprecation or intercession, as the case may be), and there are not a few who are applied to to make *guidhes* of both sorts.

We must consider the meaning of the terms used.

In South Argyllshire the common expression regarding a person or thing affected is that it is *air a chronachadh*, or, as another in Northern Argyll expressed it, *air a chronachen*. *Cron* means a fault or defect, and the verb used seems to be an expression of the opinion that something is wrong with the object, the usual meaning of the word being best translated "reproved," or "rebuked"; the speaker, as it were, finding some fault in the person or thing spoken to, he *sees* that it is faulty, and says so. In the case of a person with an Evil Eye, he actually causes defect to the object. Now the same would be true of black magic; thus, *air a chronachadh* is as apposite to a person affected by witchcraft as by the Evil Eye. It is necessary therefore to distinguish, when one hears of a case of *cronachadh*, whether it is by mischievous intention or not; and this is done sometimes by the reciter. Thus, a person consulted to cure an animal affected, when telling who it was that was to blame for the evil, said: *"Well, 'se duine le ceann dubh a chronaich do bho leis an droch shuil"* ("Well, it is a man with a black head that has injured your cow, with the Evil Eye").

In many districts this expression would merely convey the idea of rebuke (Tyree, Lewis, Dornoch, Kiltearn). In these places the expression usually is *Luidh droch shuil air* (An evil eye rested on him). In Easter Ross, a person desirous of avoiding reflections would say: *"Cha'n eil mi cuir mo shuil ann"* ("I am not putting my eye in it"). Even in Arisaig in Southern Inverness-shire, marching with Argyllshire, they use this expression only.

We have already given above, from Uist, an instance in which the speaker simply called it "the Eye," neither qualifying it as good or bad.

The rapidity of the action is sometimes expressed thus: — A healer called in, said in one case: *"Teum do bho, a bhean,"* equivalent to saying, "Your cow is bitten or stung," the word *teum* being also applied to something snatched. The operation of the Evil Eye in Uist is described by a parallel phrase, *air a ghonadh* (stabbed), an expression which has been used in Kintyre as synonymous with *cronachadh*, though there it generally expresses pain felt either bodily or mentally.

An elderly woman, a native of Duthill, Inverness-shire, while stating that there were "plenty of people round about us here who have got the Evil Eye and hurt both cattle and people with it," gave the following as the expressions used when mentioning it: —

Thuit droch shuil air (An evil eye fell on him).

Ghabh an droch shuil e (The evil eye took him).

Laidh droch shuil air (An evil eye settled on him).

Bhuail droch shuil e (An evil eye struck him).

In the part of Ireland nearest to Scotland at any rate, and so far as the writer knows also in other places, the expression used in English is "blinked." The readiest conclusion come to as to what is wrong with a sick cow is that "she has been blinked." Blinked milk, therefore, is milk which yields no butter. Blinked beer, beer which has become sour.

All these expressions, then, of the action of *an suil dona*, the common expression in part of Inverness-shire, which, seeing "Donas" is the Devil, we might translate the "diabolical eye," evidently point to the fact that a mere look will do the damage; so the remark of the Islay man, *"Ni an fheadhainn aig am bheil an t-suil so cron air beathach neo duine ged nach dean iad ach amhairc orra"* ("Those who have this eye will do injury to beast or person, though they do nothing but look on them"), expresses clearly what seems to have been the original notion conveyed in the expressions used.

A strange charm for the closure of the eye was expressed in Arran by the following saying: *"Cronachadh air do shuil, cac eun air muin sin"* ("Ill on your eye, birds' excrement on the back of that"). This was an old practice, according to the reciter, who is a woman of about eighty. The account she gave was as follows:—Her father had bought some cattle at the market. "They were fine beasts, and the servantman and I, then a young girl, were driving them home. When we were passing King's Cross a man stood and looked keenly at them. The servantman did not like this, and turning towards him said the words recited." They were avowedly used to save the cattle from being hurt by the man's eye, and as the old lady said, "Whether that saved them or no I could not tell, but in any case we reached home safely and no harm came to the cows."

The Islay expression already quoted, *Mach an dosgach*, contains within it the suggestion of evil coming to the unprotected, *Dosgadh* (calamity, misfortune), etymologically having the signification, *without protection*. [3] Subsequently we will find that no grown person need be unprotected if he will take a very small amount of trouble.

[3] Macbain, "Etymological Dictionary of the Gaelic Language."

Another Arran formula used in connection with the Evil Eye, and said to be protective, was mentioned in an account of a shepherd who lived in the island, said to have an Evil Eye. He could hurt cattle, and also cure the effect of the Evil Eye of another. The reciter said he was a queer fellow, and remembers him at the first Cattle Show ever he (reciter) attended, and being frightened by being addressed, with other boys, for being in his road: *"Mach a sin leibh. Cha'n ann airson an itheadh a tha iad"* ("Out of that with you. They are not for eating"), said the shepherd, as he drove his cattle. His mentioning eating recalled to the boys' minds his Evil Eye, and the following formula to be repeated in cases of *cronachadh*. *"Ma dh'itheas iad thu, gun sgeith iad thu, agus gun garbh sgeith iad thu"* ("If they eat you, may they vomit you, and roughly vomit you"). This seems to be chaff from non-believers to believers, possibly also the case with the formula above, more than a thing really said with a belief in its curative power.

LOCALITY OF BELIEF

There is a considerable difference between some wandering folklorist happening on a superstitious survival in some ancient crone or secluded corner, and in the general acceptation by many, if not by a majority, of some belief regarded by the more instructed as to be so classed.

The belief in the Evil Eye in the West of Scotland comes decidedly under the latter category. Interrogatories show that it exists in Caithness, Sutherland, Ross-shire, Inverness-shire, Elgin, Argyll, Perthshire, in the Lewis, Harris, both Uists, Barra, Skye, Tiree, Islay, the Isle of Man, Arran, and Antrim in Ireland. A wide enough field this. Of course there are many unbelievers, of all classes nearly, though the less the education, the more frequent the evidences of belief. An attempt to state a proportion of believers as against unbelievers is quite out of the question. One witness will tell you it was common enough in his youth, or *very common*, but in speaking of the present day, reliable witnesses will say, perhaps, most usually "pretty common," or "quite common," not unfrequently, however, "very common," or, as one unbeliever said, "you hear of them often enough." A cautious man, when you try to get exact information as to the potency of the belief, will answer that it is "strongly" held by some, and of this there can be no sort of doubt; and it is much more common than most people think.

Though we are treating of the Highlands and Islands, it must not be supposed that the "ill e'e" is a Highland speciality, speaking of Scotland alone, of course. It may with perfect sincerity be said, with all due caution, that it is "pretty common" among Lowlanders also.

SOCIAL POSITION OF BELIEVERS

The persons among whom this belief is most usual are undoubtedly to be found principally among the agricultural and fishing population, though it is not unknown, by any means, even in such a town as Oban, where a reciter of Evil Eye incidents says "it is pretty common." When one speaks of a farmer in many parts of the Low Country, one naturally thinks of well-educated men with comparatively large holdings, and such men, of course, are to be met with in the Highlands in appreciable numbers. There is no evidence that these have faith in the Evil Eye; but the smaller farmers, doing their own work with assistance, are often deeply imbued. A native of Kintyre says, "I know a respectable farmer who, when anything goes wrong with his horses, is quite in the habit of suspecting that it is injury by the Evil Eye, and will send at once for a certain woman in the neighbourhood, who is supposed to be able to cure in cases of *cronachadh*."

So lately as July 1898, in one of the islands a child was unwell. The doctor was there and the minister was there, but still the child was getting worse. At length the parents concluded that it was a case of *cronachadh*, and a man who practises as a professional in cases of that kind was sent for. On arriving he confirmed them in their suspicion, and told them that it was a woman with brown hair that had done the harm. The reciter (a minister's wife) did not know what means he took to cure the child, but whatever they were they were not successful. The child died.

Most of our beliefs are inherited, and so it is, perhaps, no wonder if one comes upon a young man, a probationer of the Church who has gone through his curriculum of study, and yet believes in the Evil Eye. No evidence, however, is forthcoming of a licensed medical man having any belief in it. It must be admitted that the greater part of the information is got from women, and if believers were polled, the majority would be found of the less stern sex.

From the small farmer downwards, among all owners of stock, and this includes chickens and the pig, believers are frequent.

In some places there is but little secrecy as to those who have the Evil Eye, or at least are supposed to have it. We refrain from publishing the full names, so that if by any chance those spoken of see this they may not be offended; but this is a sample of a common style of remark: "*Tha, tha, tha droch shuil aig Anna nic E. Nach robh Mrs. MacT. ag innseadh dhomh fhein nach bu mhor nach robh aon da clann marbh le droch shuil a' bhoirionnach sin uair. Bha e air a chronachadh leatha, agus bhitheadh e marbh ach airson Anna T.*" ("Yes, yes, Ann McE. has an Evil Eye. Was not Mrs. MacT. telling myself that one of her children was once nearly dead through the Evil Eye of that woman. He was injured by her, and would have been dead had it not been for Ann T.") Ann T. was a practitioner of *eolas*.

DESCRIPTION OF POSSESSORS OF EVIL EYE

Anybody may have the Evil Eye, but that certain people suggest the Evil Eye to others from their appearance must be admitted. A minister, himself a son of the manse, who has had Highland surroundings all his early life, bears witness, "The possession was more frequently ascribed to females than to males, and for the most part to elderly women." Another minister, an older man than the former, says of the Evil Eye: "They were chiefly women that were suspected, and were generally much disliked in the communities." These two reciters were as far apart as Arran and Ross-shire.

Was the Evil Eye ascribed to them because they were disliked, or were they disliked because they had the Evil Eye? Women do not improve in appearance with age, nor men either, for the matter of that, and one of our reciters, in describing a case of *cronachadh,* said that the operator was "a bad-looking woman at any rate, and had a queer look." In Knapdale we hear of one who was "a decent enough looking woman, but there was this about her, people always suspected her of having some evil power, and nobody liked to refuse her if she asked anything." Another of the accused was "strange in her dress, and spoke in an imperious manner."

It is curious to note that, having quoted all the descriptions of individuals we have, the criticisms should all be levelled at women; but it must not be supposed that men are at all exempt. The writer was amused, and not a little astonished, to hear that an old gentleman, a connection of his own, a large farmer and not unknown beyond his own district, certainly not a greedy man, and a pleasant companion, was among some as notorious for his Evil Eye as for his knowledge of his business. He was a Low Country man by descent, ignorant of Gaelic, and surrounded by Gaelic-speaking Highlanders, some of whom however, proprietors and taxmen, were said to be as bad as himself.

The only diagnostic mark that has been mentioned, physically demonstrating a possessor, was got from an Islay woman, who said that she had always heard that a person whose eyes are of a different colour has the

Evil Eye. This seems explicable enough; if one were a nice bright blue eye or a deep and gentle brown one, and the other paler and less expressive, their best friends might say that they had a "bad eye." All the parti-coloured eyes in Scotland would not account for a tenth part of the results accredited to evil eyes.

Small are the changes in the ideas of men in some respects, even after long intervals.

In the old Irish saga, entitled the *Sack of Da Derga's Hostel*, describing events which occurred, according to the Irish analysts, either b.c. 31, or a.d. 43: [4] "When they were there they saw a lone woman coming to the door of the hostel, after sunset, and seeking to be let in. As long as a weaver's beam was each of her two shins, and they were as dark as the back of a stag-beetle. A greyish, woolly mantle she wore. Her lower hair used to reach as far as her knee. Her lips were on one side of her head. She came and put one of her shoulders against the door-post of the house, casting the Evil Eye on the King and the youths who surrounded him in the hostel." [5]

[4] Translated by Whitley Stokes, *Revue Celtique*, vol. xxii. p. 12.

[5] Whitley Stokes, *Revue Celtique*, xxii. pp. 57-59. The existing redaction of within saga is certainly as old as the tenth century.

The Gaelic word translated by Stokes here "casting the Evil Eye" is in the original Gaelic "*oc admilliud ind rig,*" literally to this day "hurting or spoiling the king," *cronachadh,* in fact. It says nothing of incantations or magical observances, and the translation given seems thoroughly justified. The description of Cailb, Samon, Sinand (she was the possessor of many names), of course imaginatively exaggerates her ugliness, but her evil looks, with her black fire-burned shins, is just what one would expect to hear of an old woman credited with the Evil Eye nowadays, though it is not now common to expose so much leg as to show the effect of toasting it at the fire.

One can easily fancy that the warriors of Ireland would have no pleasure in encountering Cailb. A like objection is common in the present day in regard to persons with an Evil Eye.

A Western Islander says: "People would be blaming J. B., but there was one worse than her. Nobody who ever met M. McA. when on his way to fish, would go on, for it was believed that no fish would be got after meeting her." The reciter himself and another man were on their way to fish when they met this woman. The other suggested that there was no use going now, for they would not get anything, that was sure. The reciter said that he grudged turning back, although he believed his companion was right; but not to waste time, and to avoid the chance of other mischief, they both returned home.

"J. McE. was said to have the Evil Eye, and no one liked to meet her if they were going on important business, especially to fish; some would even turn back if they met her."

OBJECTION TO MEETING AN EVIL EYE

Another informant, speaking of a woman with an Evil Eye and who consequently was unlucky to meet, said: "Three fishermen met her, and one of them proposed that they should turn back; it was no use going on, they would get nothing. The others persisted and overruled him. They were for a while unsuccessful, and he who had proposed returning was very impatient, and kept grumbling and saying they should have returned home. They did catch a few at last."

Speaking of those who were supposed to take the milk and butter from other people's cows, an educated Arran man said: "This class were looked upon as being unlucky to meet on the road, and people tried to avoid them, especially if they were going on any particular business."

One would suppose that it would be exceedingly unpleasant to have the reputation of an Evil Eye, consequently it is resented, but precautions are taken sometimes, even before the accusation is made, to hinder the report arising about individuals. In one village, where twice a week a number of fishermen pass, the women and girls of the village try to keep out of sight of the men on their way to the fishing-ground, lest, if by chance a fisher should see one of them and he was unlucky immediately thereafter, he would report to the rest his want of luck and whom he had met, and she would be marked as one of the unlucky.

The reciter of this was an intelligent domestic servant, twenty-four years old, a reliable girl, brought up by respectable grandparents.

A Kintyre reciter, an educated woman of about thirty, informs us of a woman, a believer in the Evil Eye, living beside her father, and who does not conceal the fact that she looks with some suspicion upon certain of her acquaintances should they come her way, particularly should she be engaged in churning. Her neighbours, knowing this, are careful to avoid going to her house if she has a churning on hand. Suspected persons do not learn their own infirmity merely by being looked at askance.

A clergyman in one of the southern islands informs us: "It is said that in cases where injury has been done by the Evil Eye, a remedy is to charge the suspected party firmly and distinctly to his (or her) face with having done it. When a little boy, a cow belonging to his grandmother had lately calved, and a neighbour woman came one day and went to see the cow. She was considered to be a respectable person, even a good woman, but was believed to possess the Evil Eye. She was no time away when the cow became very unwell, although there had been nothing wrong with her up till then. There was considerable excitement, and they were sure that the cow would die, and just as sure it was the woman's Evil Eye that had injured her. Another woman was sent for, supposed to be knowing in these matters, and the case submitted to her. She confirmed them in their suspicions, and advised, as the best remedy, that she who had done the mischief should be confronted and plainly told to her face that they believed her to be to blame. This was agreed to and carried out at once, with the result, as it was believed, that whatever power she had obtained over the cow to hurt her was broken, and in a very short time the cow was as well as she had ever been."

An Arran woman tells us the same thing in some detail, but she says the injury can only be repaired by the doer of the mischief taking upon himself the evil done to the other, and illustrates it by the following story:—A tramp who was supposed to have a bad eye, and even suspected of witchcraft, made a request to Mrs. Mac—— which she refused. The woman being angered, left in a rage. She was no time away when they noticed that there was something wrong with the child, and when the husband came from his work his wife told him of the woman having been there, and her belief that she had injured their child. The man said the woman was still in the neighbourhood, and he would bring her back. He did so. They then charged her to her face with having hurt the child, and said she must now heal her. The woman did not try to deny this, but said: *"Tha e gle chruaidh gum feumainnsa an cron a rinn mi air an leanabh agaibh a ghabhail orm fein, ach na'n d'thug sibhse bonn airgeid dhomhsa an ait' an olann a thug sibh dhomh, cha do thachair so do'n leanabh"* ("It's very hard that I should require to take on myself the injury I have done your child, but if you had given me a silver coin instead of the wool you gave me, this had not happened to the child").

She had to cure the child, however. What had happened to it was that its mouth kept always open, and it could not catch the breast. The reciter did not say that the malady of the open mouth stuck to the woman, but being somewhat notorious, and a different incident being told of her by another reciter, the latter remarked that "she had an ungainly face, and that if ever there was a witch in Arran, he thought that woman would pass for one."

AVOIDING SUSPICION OF EVIL EYE

People have not always the candour to accuse the suspected.

A lady engaged in teaching gives the following information: "You would hear of Mrs. McG.? She is making a great noise because, as she says, the milk is being taken from her cow, and not long ago her horse and some other beast of hers died, and she thinks it is because they were *air an cronachadh* by some person. She blamed a girl that was keeping house with a neighbour, and she went to the girl's sister and said to her to say to her sister not to be taking away the milk from her cow." This was not supposed to be a case of witchcraft.

So far we have been dealing with women, but it must not be supposed that such accusations are rarely made against men.

A small farmer, Alexander — —, having got into difficulties, lost his farm. A neighbour, better able to stock it, entered into possession. Soon, however, a cow died, and it was concluded that it was a case of *cronachadh*, an opinion in which its owner agreed, declaring: "*Well, cho fad's bhios bo bheo agam, cha dean mise rithist namhaid de Alasdair*" ("Well, as long as I have a living cow I will not again make an enemy of Alexander").

Men are also as cautious to avoid suspicion as women. Recently a servant-girl in Islay, having the charge of attending to the feeding of a pig, requested a man who had never been suspected of possessing a hurtful eye to look at the pig to see how it was thriving. The man refused, adding quite seriously that he did not like to look at a beast that way, in case of any harm being done. When she persisted that there could be no harm, he replied that not long ago M. McL. had a litter of young pigs, and a man came that way and was looking at them one evening, and the next morning they were all dead.

The reasons ascribed for the action of some are doubtless influenced by the reciter's own beliefs. Thus, it was often said of a gentleman farmer in Rothiemurchus, well known in the countryside, that he would never praise any beast of his own, and this was supposed to be owing to his belief that he himself had an Evil Eye. It does not seem to have occurred to his neighbours that it was native modesty.

To show the hold that belief in an Evil Eye has on certain minds, a native of Ross-shire tells how he went to see a neighbour, who asked his assistance in putting a ring in the nose of a pig to prevent it rooting. "There was another neighbour of his there too, who had come forward when he saw us, one W. M., an intelligent man, and one that I would never have thought would give in to these superstitions; but he was a man that believed in the Evil Eye, although nobody suspected him of having it himself." Accidentally the pig's leg was broken. It was understood to belong to the wife of the man who proposed to ring it, who said:—

"Man, what will we say to the wife? But come away in and see what she has got to say." When we went in the wife asked us if we had got the ring in the pig, and her man answered, "No, and I am sorry to tell you the pig has broken her leg."

"How did that happen?" she asked, and her husband said, out of pure fun, "Oh, I don't know, unless W. M.'s eye has fallen upon her." That was enough. Up W. got in a wild rage, and said he would not sit under such a suspicion, and off he marched, terribly offended.

At the time of writing a reciter, a woman, admits that at K. in A. a man is living whom his neighbours believe to have the Evil Eye, and people not only do not like to meet him, but go out of their way to avoid him when going on important matters. It is told of him that a donkey belonging to a woman kicked his horse. The donkey's owner expressed a hope that he would not come to know of it, lest he should hurt her beast. Her fear was justified, as it turned out, for the man saw the donkey kick the horse, and however he managed it, people believed that he put *cronachadh* on the donkey, for it turned ill and shortly died.

ACTION OF EVIL EYE INDEPENDENT OF POSSESSOR

It must be difficult, one would think, for any reasonably kindly-intentioned person to accept as proved that they had an Evil Eye. But a distinction is made between possessing an Evil Eye and doing mischief with it. A native of Glen Urquhart, Inverness-shire, among others says that there it is understood a person may possess an Evil Eye and do mischief with it without intending it, and without knowing that he has done it. When a person knows that he has an Evil Eye, and does mischief with it intentionally, the ill-doing is usually supposed to be more or less connected with witchcraft.

Many believe the injury from the Evil Eye is quite independent of the will of the possessor. A farmer, a believer, said: "When we were in the old place more than thirty years ago, there was a man living upon the hill who would often be helping the farmers round about when they were throng. He had the Evil Eye; but he could not help it. He would be sorry for it himself; many a one would be scolding him for hurting their beasts."

Another says: "*Cronachadh* is still in it, and those that have got the Evil Eye cannot help it. They sometimes do harm with their eye when they do not intend it, and even when they do not know that they are doing it."

This seems a thoroughly rooted idea in Islay, and a Tiree man informs us that there it is also thought that injury by an Evil Eye is involuntary on the part of the person who has such an eye, and not necessarily malicious or intended.

This is also met with as a belief in Arran, and a reciter there tells of a minister in the Parish of Kilmory who had the Evil Eye in spite of himself, and if he looked on his own cattle or horses they were sure to be ill after. Other cases are mentioned, and one of our reciters told how a man, while resident in the south of the island, and fond of fine cattle, in the place where he was well known and respected had never been suspected of the Evil Eye, but removing to the Whiting Bay district, where he was among strangers, suspicion of the Evil Eye attached to him and remained with him to the day of his death.

In these two last cases, in speculating upon the cause of the accusation, it seems quite probable that the minister, being occupied with his own special duties, rarely regarded the state of his beasts, and only took notice of them under exceptional circumstances, and coincidence had connected his inspection of them and their illnesses. The other evidently was an amateur with an eye to beauty in others' cattle, and probably had unfortunately expressed approval before subsequent misfortune. One notorious incident was undoubtedly enough to set the report going, and all know the results of giving a lie half-an-hour's start.

EVIL EYE TAKES EFFECT EVEN ON THINGS NOT SEEN

There is one simple way of keeping your property safe from the Evil Eye: viz., by not letting it be known that you have what may be affected. A certain D. MacF., who knew that his neighbour was crediting his Evil Eye with having spoiled a churning, was standing in the back-yard when the woman who suspected him was milking her cow. She, having finished, should have passed him with her milk to carry it in by the door, but on seeing him she started, and instead of coming forward, passed the pitcher of milk in by a little window on the back wall of the house, and then walked forward and went in at the door, passing MacF. He concluded that her object was to keep the milk out of his sight lest he should hurt it. MacF. disavows the possession of any power of the kind.

Another reciter mentions that a certain Calum Ban, having the name of the Evil Eye, others kept things out of his sight for fear that he might hurt them.

The mere preventing the eye resting on the thing to be affected would, however, have been quite insufficient, according to one reciter, a native of Bernera (Harris). She told of one, recognised as possessing an Evil Eye, that he was sure to covet everything in the possession of his neighbours, and consequently "those nearest R. were very unfortunate." His influence was understood to extend beyond what he actually saw, and therefore even hearing about things was kept from him. On one occasion the young daughter of R.'s neighbour set eggs under two hens, and being considered "lucky," having usually been successful, she expected two good broods. In the interval she mentioned what she had done in the hearing of R.'s daughter. When the time came not a single chicken appeared out of the two settings. Her mother then said she would put eggs below the hens, but warned all in the house to be sure and not tell that they were there. This was done, the hens being kept carefully concealed, and full and thriving broods were got.

An old man now dead, a crofter who could read, who was strongly superstitious, telling his stories with great gusto, and reliable, is the authority for the following, which shows how the superstitions of others were played on. In the time when ploughs were made of wood of a home manufacture, the farmer in Octofad brought home a new one. One day, using the new plough, coming round at the end of a furrow, the plough was broken in two. The man between the stilts and the man leading the horses threw the blame of the carelessness on one another. At last the latter proposed that if the ploughman would leave to him to tell the old man (the farmer) how it happened, and if he would not say a word at all in the matter, he believed that he would be able to put it past (*a chuir seachad*) right enough. The ploughman agreed. They took the horses home, and when the farmer made his appearance looking displeased (*coslas gu math crosda air*), the lad began his tale. "*De ach am beist duine sin tha ann C. aig am bheil an droch shuil. Thainig e an rathad far an robh sin a treabhadh, agus on a bhios a shuil aige anns gach ni a chi e, thoisich e air a bhi moladh nan each agus a chrann; agus cha robh e tiota air falbh, nuair a chaidh a' chrann ann an da leth.*" ("What but that beast of a man that is in C., who has the Evil Eye. He came the way where we were ploughing, and since he will have his eye in everything he sees, he began praising the horses and the plough, and he was no time gone when the plough went in two halves.")

The lad's forecast was correct. His master's eye lost its gloom, and shaking his hand to them, he said: "Never mind, never mind; put in the horses, and do not say a word about it to anybody in case he may do more harm. If the horses are safe, we will not be long in dressing the plough."

It is perfectly clear that an interesting instance of the influence of the Evil Eye was established here, so far as the farmer was concerned, and doubtless the belief in it generally owes not a little to equally fanciful stories.

MORAL SOURCE OF THE EVIL EYE

Though the action of the Evil Eye is accepted as involuntary, in the majority of cases, this is not the accepted doctrine in all districts. From Ross-shire (Strathpeffer) a reciter says:—

"It is a power which they are in some cases supposed to exercise involuntarily, but oftener intentionally and with mischievous design."

From somewhat the same locality, Dores (near Inverness), a reciter "thinks that the involuntary kind that is often met with in certain other parts of the Highlands is not recognised, but in every case in which injury arises from an Evil Eye, it is to be referred to active covetousness and greed of gain at other people's expense." But even in Kintyre, where the involuntary action is accepted, a native tells us: "I believe in what people call the Evil Eye, and I have known very many who believed in it just as much as I do; not that every man has it, for there are only some that I would be afraid of. If I see a man that thinks highly of what belongs to himself, and would not exchange it with any man, that is the man I would like to have dealings with, for although he might do injury to himself, or to any living thing he might possess, he would do no harm to another. If I saw a man envying everything he saw, and thinking what belonged to other people was better than what belonged to himself, I would be afraid of that man, and if I had cattle I would not like him to come among them, for if he came I would be sure something would happen."

A Mull woman said: "*Cronachadh* is quite common. It is done usually by a person that has an Evil Eye. It is just an eye with great greed and envy."

An Islay man says: "*Tha cronachadh ann. Se 'n droch cridhe tha dol thun na sul, agus a' deanadh droch suil.*" ("*Cronachadh* exists. It is the evil heart going to the eye and causing an Evil Eye.") The suggestion thus is that an Evil Eye is but the result of the natural man who has not rooted out of his nature what is forbidden in the Tenth Commandment, and so a native of Ross-shire (Tarbat) shows how strong the belief was that mischief might come "through the Evil Eye or ill wish of another." A certain aunt of his formed a strong dislike to him when he was a boy, simply because it was known that his grandfather favoured him to the disadvantage of this aunt, as she thought, and he well remembered how anxious his mother was for a long time, lest the aunt's known ill-will should cause some blight to come on him.

The following from Islay shows that though the belief there that it is involuntary is strongly held, those who have the power may exercise it deliberately. "There was a woman in Islay who had a sow that had a litter of young pigs. One morning a neighbour came to her, and seeing the teapot at the fire, asked if she would give her a drop of the tea. This was given to her. She then said, 'You have fine young pigs there.' 'Yes, but they are all sold,' answered the other. With that the visitor turned towards the door to go, and said, 'Well, you sold a pig to me that died.' That was all that passed, and she went her way; but the following morning two of the pigs were dead, and the owner was quite certain that the woman had done the mischief. The reciter who gives the information is of the same opinion, and he adds that it was an unkind thing to do on a poor woman."

The strength of the Evil Eye, according to some, is to be gauged by the following remark by an old man: "*B'abhaist gu'm biodh e air a radh le sean daoine, gun sgoilteadh an t-suil sanntach eadhon na creagan fein o cheile.*" ("It used to be said by old people that the greedy eye would split asunder the very rocks.")

Another says *cronachadh* is just envy, and it is said that envy will break the very stones. A man who wishes to have everything for himself will do harm to whatever he sees.

THINGS THAT SPECIALLY ATTRACT

A woman of twenty-eight, whose information is quite reliable, the daughter of a respectable man in one of the inner islands, remembers when young people talked a great deal about these things, and many were very much afraid of them. "The idea was that it was always the best and prettiest of beast or body that was most liable to be injured by a bad eye. Her youngest brother was awfully pretty when a child. They used to have him dressed in a red frock and white pinny, and with his fair skin, fair curly hair, and red cheeks, he was the nicest-looking child in all the place. Many a time, when my father would take him out, the neighbours would be warning him to take good care lest some one might do the child harm, and some would advise my father to go in and take the frock and pinny off him, so that he might not draw one's attention so much."

From Ross-shire we hear the same thing. A native "remembers when he was young, people believed in the Evil Eye and were afraid of it." It was supposed that pretty children were specially liable to be injured by it, and it was a common device with some mothers, in circumstances where there was any suspicion of danger, to take care that at least some article of the child's dress would be at fault, either in respect of neatness or cleanness, or better still, to have one of the child's stockings turned outside in when being worn. These were supposed to form a protection to the child against injury.

The reciter remembers quite well a woman who in her own person and house was the pink of neatness, but full of superstition, and he cannot remember ever having seen her children without something untidy about them. Always a stocking or something else wrong on, and this was done intentionally by their mother to keep away the Evil Eye.

A native of Bernera (Harris) testified: "When a person appears well dressed and good-looking, it is supposed that she is in danger of being affected by the Evil Eye. A recommendation in such a case is to wear some article of clothing with the wrong side out, as a preventative of harm."

An old man of eighty-seven, uneducated, but full of information, somewhat difficult to understand from the loss of his teeth and the weakness of his voice, telling his experiences in the most pathetic manner, said: "*Bu nighean a' cheud duine cloinne bha riomh agam, agus bha deigh mhor agam oirre. Ach de thachair, ach latha bha 'n sin, bha i amach aig taobh an tighe, agus bha neach a' dol seachad aig an robh droch shuil, agus chaidh an droch shuil anns an leanabh, agus bha i air a chronachadh. O'n am sin chaidh an creatur air a h-ais co mor gus aig a cheann mu dheireadh cha robh i air a cumail beo ach le beagan fion a bha air a chuir ann a beul le spain ti."* ("The first one of my family was a daughter. She was a pretty child, and I was very fond of her. But what happened but a day that was there, she was out at the side of the house and a person passed who had an Evil Eye, and the Evil Eye went into the child and she was injured. From that time the creature went back so much, until at last she was only kept alive by a little wine put into her mouth with a teaspoon.")

"When people had occasion to go to farmer R.'s house, having children with them, they contrived to put some attractive article of clothing on the children, so that the gay clothes might divert his eye from the wearers and save them from injury."

A native of Knockando (Elgin) says that there is an impression that the young, either of man or beast, are very liable to receive injury from an Evil Eye fastening upon them, if that should be the first eye that sees them after their birth. This belief makes people take great care often to secure that any one supposed to possess an Evil Eye will not be the first to see an infant immediately after birth, or any other young animal.

Using short texts separated from the context leads undoubtedly to misapprehensions on the part of the unlearned. In Isaiah xiii. 18, he says of the Medes, alluding to physical injury alone, "their eye shall not spare children." That text has influenced not a few.

Without any suspicion of the owner of a beast having the Evil Eye himself, his desire to retain it is supposed to render it specially liable to the evil influence of any one possessed of the power. A Kinlochbervie man remembers well how very common, in his youth, was belief in the Evil Eye, and vividly recalls the terror his mother had when any unknown vagrant came the way, lest, being possessed of an Evil Eye, he might leave a blight on the house or anything belonging to it. She would give almost anything they might ask so as to get them away in a good mood.

STRANGERS SPECIALLY LIABLE TO BE ACCUSED OF THE POSSESSION OF THE EVIL EYE

Acquaintances might be divided into two classes. The Evil Eyes and the Non-Evil Eyes. Precautions should be taken against the former, and with them it was safe to class strangers. The daughter of a tradesman, a clever, intelligent woman, a farmer's wife, whose husband's people and her own mother are very superstitious, having moved from one district to another, her new neighbours, not long after she had came to live beside them, lost a number of geese. The owners made a great "ado," and the position they took up relative to our reciter, the suspected one, was: "*Faicibh fein an droch shuil tha aice. Cha deachaidh na geoidh air seachran riomh roimhe, ach ghabh iad fuath 'nuair a' dh' amhairc ise orra.*" ("See for yourself the Evil Eye she had; the geese never before wandered, but took fright when she looked at them.")

The owners of these geese seem to have had a very lively faith in the Evil Eye. The collector having mentioned the experience to another neighbour, she said: "That's not so bad as I got. I went to inquire for a friend if they would sell a goose. They said they would not sell, and there was no harm in that; but shortly after all the geese flew away, and if I did not catch it. They were in a fearful rage, blaming me for putting my Evil Eye in them. Another time their hens ceased laying, and they blamed my eye for that also."

It is scarcely to be wondered at, the jealous ascription of the Evil Eye to strangers, though Highland publications speak largely of the noble characteristics of Highlanders at large, and the writer is the last man to deny them credit due. It must be confessed there is a large quantity of a 'parochial' feeling of jealousy in the Highlands generally. It is not necessary to go into the question whether this is or is not the modern aspect of previous district quarrels. Tramps trade upon this fear of strangers in other Gaelic places than the Scottish Highlands. A minister relates the following, which came under his own observation in Antrim. A tramp was passing a house, and he went and asked the housewife for a drink of milk. She said she had no milk, but the tramp was sure she had, but did not want to part with it. He said, "Oh, very well, I'll take a drink of water, and let what will happen to the cows." This was enough; she was sure that this was a challenge that he would have the milk in spite of her, so she repented and gave him as good a drink of milk as he could wish for, no doubt in this way escaping evil consequences.

PEOPLE SHOULD GIVE WHEN ASKED

The danger of refusing a request is great, not so much from the purely Christian-charity point of view, as from that of escaping the Evil Eye. A native of Knapdale, a believer, tells of a woman notorious in that neighbourhood. She went to a farmer for a barrel of potatoes, which he refused her. No more was said, but she had not long gone when the best horse he had fell down and could not rise. It was foaming at the mouth. A man skilled in counteracting the Evil Eye was consulted, and declared that the horse had been injured by it. Having been informed by the farmer that he had refused to give a barrel of potatoes to the woman, he said it was that that had done the harm. His advice was a little peculiar, not in that he recommended the sending the potatoes to the woman, but that they should be sent on the injured horse, with evidently a view to its cure. The potatoes were got into a bag, the bag lifted on the horse's back, and away it went quite briskly, and they were delivered at the woman's house, and thereafter the horse was quite well.

Drovers are not, of course, complete strangers in the districts in which they do business, but as a class they are looked on with some suspicion. Thus we are told, "Some drovers are possessed of the Evil Eye, and in consequence it is reckoned foolish not to sell any animals to them if they appear anxious to have them." The reciter's father had a good cow, and some drovers coming about wanted to buy her. His father refused to sell. The drovers persisted, but still met with a refusal. At last the drovers left, but shortly after the cow sickened, died, and nothing remained of her value to the owner but her skin.

A parallel case was mentioned as happening in Islay. "I remember it was a few days before the market a man came the way and wanted to buy a beast from A. McI. The drover was very anxious to get it, but they would not sell. The drover left, and before the sun went down that evening that beast was dead and buried. The reciter of this, a man of about fifty and a good workman, living by himself, is a piper, and possibly the addition of the beast's hurried burial may be the result of a natural tendency to 'blow,' as they say. Anyhow, the piper said that it was believed that it was the drover's eye that had killed the cow."

Another reciter tells that a farmer in Islay had two good horses which some dealers wished to buy. The farmer would not sell either, and the following day one of them died. It was believed to be a case of Evil Eye.

The risk of refusing purchasers is not solely in the case of drovers. "Many are of opinion that it is risky for a person to refuse to sell any animal he may have to any one who shows a great desire to purchase it; some would sell at a sacrifice rather than run the risk. A native of Killean, Kintyre, tells of a fine cow his father had, and on which the family set a considerable value. A man who had known something about the cow came all the way from Campbeltown purposely to buy her, but the owner declined to sell her. "If he did, he hardly got any good of her thereafter, for in a short time she became unwell, and lingering for a time, died. The neighbours thought it was a real case of Evil Eye."

From the mainland of Argyllshire a lady relates: "An uncle had a farm five miles from Oban. A neighbour on his way to attend a funeral, thinking her uncle might drive along with him, called. As he was passing the cow-fold the calves were being let out to their mothers, and one of the cows had a beautiful calf. The neighbour fixed his eyes on them and kept looking at and admiring them. He then asked her uncle if he would sell him the calf, but the proprietor refused, saying he did not intend to sell either cow or calf. That very week the calf was dead, and they never doubted but that it was the man's Evil Eye that had killed it."

A native of Applecross in Ross-shire told he had bought a fine horse, but before the purchase another man had been looking at it and been very anxious to have it, and praised it as a splendid beast. It was not long in the reciter's possession until it had some complaint from which it died. The people—the reciter does not himself say he shares the feeling—believe that it was killed by the Evil Eye, for it had been known to everybody how anxious the disappointed man had been to get it, and how highly he had spoken of it.

SYMPTOMS IN ANIMALS ASCRIBED TO EFFECT OF EVIL EYE

One naturally asks what are the symptoms which, when present in animals, have given rise to the supposition that they were affected by the Evil Eye.

A woman gives the following account of what happened to her mother. She had been married very young, and was sitting by the fire suckling her first child with her breasts bare. The child had fallen asleep on her left arm. "My mother heard something behind her, and when she turned her head, there was a tall, grey-haired, ill-favoured-looking woman standing. My mother got up hurriedly, and having a great deal of milk, the milk spouted from her right breast into the fire. The *cailleach* gave an unpleasant laugh and said, 'The milk has gone along with the pee.' My mother answered pleasantly enough, 'Oh no, the milk and pee will be all right,' and gave the *cailleach* what she wanted. She was a Tiree *cailleach*, and they were all looked upon as being bad ones. The next time my mother was going to give her baby a drink she found she had not a drop of milk for him. The baby was crying, and when he would cry she would cry too, and what was to be done? This state of things lasted for a day, and my father then went for assistance from a person supposed to be skilled."

The expression used by the Tiree woman was understood by the reciter to mean the milk that should have nourished the child was to turn into water in the mother's system, and be so discharged.

Yawning has been ascribed to the effect of the Evil Eye.

An Islay man said: "*Bha piuthair aig an te nach maireann agus bha i cho boidheach 'sa chunnaic sibh riomh. Aon uair thainig boireannach a stigh agus thoiseach i air a chaileag a mholadh gu ro mhor. Well, cha robh a bhean sin ach gann air dol amach nur a thoiseach a chaileag air meunanaich, agus cha robh fad gus an robh i cho dona agus gun robh iad a saoilsinn gum bitheadh i air falbh.*"

("My late wife had a sister, and she was as pretty as ever you saw. Once a woman came in and commenced praising the girl excessively. Well, scarcely was that woman gone out of the house when the girl began to yawn, and it was not long till she was so bad that they thought that she would be away (die).")

In the case of a child which was quite quiet and looking well, with the mother sitting nursing it, a neighbouring woman, who is not much liked in the place, came in. She sat a little while, and was no time away until the child began to cry. It cried long and bitterly, and its mother got into a fearful state, protesting of the other woman: "*Co fior's tha mi beo, chronaich i mo phaisde*" ("As true as I am alive she injured my child"). It is interesting to note that in this case "a little white powder" prescribed by a qualified practitioner counteracted that Evil Eye.

Another case in which a child was ill was told as follows:—A woman went to inquire after a man who had just lost his wife in the Low Country, and brought their child home to his relations. She was told that the child was "not but poorly." "What is the matter with him?" I asked. My informant answered me, that his mother had been sitting at the fire and the child in her bosom, when two women came to ask for the child's father. The child was quite well and brisk when they came in, but before they went away he began to cry and groan. "He was quite sure," he said, "that one or other of them had injured the child, but why they should do that he did not know, for they both had families of their own." This case was cured by an unlicensed practitioner.

The following is from a woman of her own experience in the case of her own son. She told that his sister went out with him one day to a neighbour's house. He was sitting in her lap, when the neighbour's daughter called her mother's attention to the white beauty of the child's legs. The mother agreed, and something more was said praising the child, and he then got a drink of milk. Well, as soon as he took the milk, he began as if he were singing, "Do re do, do re do." This he continued to do for a good while, and was very fretful. This child was cured by a magic thread which stopped the "humming."

Cattle, in popular belief, are much more liable to damage from the Evil Eye than other animals, judging from the greater number of instances related of it in their case. "Two of M. McN.'s cattle died within a short time of each other, and all the old people of the place persisted in saying they were injured by some Evil Eye." A reciter told of her mother, who had married the elder of two brothers occupying a farm in common, getting the credit of the Evil Eye because, shortly after her marriage, the cattle on the farm "began to die right away."

In the following case motive is given, and if any overt act of a magical nature had been said to occur, it would certainly have to be classified as witchcraft, but seeing there is no such history, it is one of those cases in which the action of an Evil Eye was evidently not supposed to be involuntary. The heir to a tenant who had fallen into arrears, having paid what was owing, got possession from the superior. Meanwhile a woman had been living in the house. She was warned to leave, but paid no heed to the warning, and it became necessary to turn her out by force. She got shelter from a relative near by, while the new tenant went to live in the house from which she had been ejected. "But if he did, he soon suffered for it, for he was not long there until he had lost nine of his cattle by death, and he and every one else believed that they had been "*air an cronachadh*" by the woman from spite.

There are no symptoms recounted in these general losses.

More rarely than of cows, we hear of stirks being affected. This is rather an old story, and the authority for this is the reciter's father, who told it of his own father. He was at market in Stratherrick, and refused to part, after considerable bargaining, with a stirk he had to a would-be buyer. "Before the market-day closed, down fell the stirk on the ground and nothing could make it get up."

In a quite recent case, however, a stirk, said to be affected by the Evil Eye, "was very ill; its horns were quite cold, and it could not eat anything. The beast recovered."

By far most commonly, evil from a "bad eye" comes to cows. A reciter tells of an instance that occurred to himself, where in a farm previously occupied, his mother had a particularly good cow. "One day my sister was in a neighbour's house, and she was telling the woman about the lot of milk this cow had. The next day when my mother went out at the usual hour to milk the cow, she had scarcely begun when this woman passed close to where she was milking. Well, not a drop of milk could my mother get from that cow. The cow became suddenly unwell and fell to the ground. The skin came off her udder and not a bit of skin was on it after that. There was not the least doubt but that it was the other woman that had injured her."

A native of Skye, in whose younger days the belief in the Evil Eye was very common there, and who remembers seeing "a general turn up" in the township in which she was brought up, caused by the alleged effect of one person's Evil Eye upon the cattle of the neighbours, tells how her father had a fine Ayrshire cow. She was such a good milker that it was necessary to milk her three times every day. "All of a sudden her milk left her, and they never could account for it, except on the supposition of the action of an Evil Eye, and in fact were quite sure that this was the case."

The reciter of the following says she remembers a Sutherlandshire minister telling it to her mother. He said that one time his cows were not giving the right milk. The milk was more like water than milk, and as for butter, not a bit could he get, no matter how well it might be churned. The minister here, on the advice of his housekeeper, resorted to witchcraft for a cure.

Another reciter says: "When my sister and myself were lumps of lasses we were down the road one day with a cow of my father's. When we brought her home the milk was running from her, and she lay down on the floor and she wouldn't rise. When they tried to put her up she would make as if she would climb up the wall."

In fact, as another reciter in Rothiemurchus said: "It used to be a very common experience to have cows going off their milk, and sometimes dying from the effects of a person possessed of an Evil Eye looking upon them, and it is still believed that cases of this kind happen."

A cow that was "kicking and would let nobody milk her," being cured by one of the processes against the Evil Eye, the cure was understood to certify the diagnosis.

Mrs. McN. was milking her cow. A woman passing at the time remarked, looking at the cow the while, "That is a grand cow, and she gives a great deal of milk." "Yes, she is a good cow," replied the owner, and the woman having passed on there was no more about it, until a little while after the milking was done the cow lay down on the ground and began to roll in great pain. There never was any doubt but that it was a case of injury by the Evil Eye. The cow was cured by magic.

Another cow "grew to be unwell, and she was rolling herself upon the ground." She was so unwell that the schoolmaster, who was a great friend of her owner's, advised him to send for a man to flay her. She recovered.

Of course a recognised wizard may have the Evil Eye as much as a more innocent person. The reciter of this, a credulous man, no doubt, and uneducated, with the gift of the gab and a good deal of natural shrewdness, a distillery workman, is detailing his own experience. "The cows were all tied in the byre, and we were looking in the window and saw the *Buidseach ruadh* (the red wizard) standing at the byre door. The door was in two halves, the upper half was open at the time, the lower closed, and he was leaning on it and gazing with all his might at one of the cows. The kitchen was at the end of the byre, and they always came straight down from the kitchen when they were going to milk. The women just came down then, and when they came to the cow that he had been looking at, not a drop of milk could they get. When they untied her to let her out she gave a loud bellow, and running up by the kitchen door made for the fire and tried to go up by the chain through the roof of the house. They had nothing for it but tie her up again, and for some days they did not get a drop of milk from her, and her skin became so loose on her it looked as if hardly sticking to her flesh at all. When the day for churning came they found the butter was gone also."

A Kintyre man recites the following of an authority consulted for the cure of the Evil Eye. "Her cow, put out for the first time after calving, became wild and jumped against everything like to kill herself. There was nothing for it but just to put her back into the house. Everybody was sure the beast had been *air a cronachadh* by some person's Evil Eye, or bewitched by witchcraft. When the woman to whom the cow belonged came to know of it she came up, and going up to the cow, gave her a clap or two on the back, said something, and in a minute or two the cow was as quiet as she had ever been."

A farmer of the name of M. had the farm of B., near Campbeltown. He had a favourite cow which he would not part with for anything. Some drovers wished to buy this cow, but M. refused, and though the drovers persisted, he would not part with her. They went to the cow and began to soothe and fondle her. When they left the cow began to go about in a circle, and could not be got out of that circle. At length the farmer was forced to kill her. This was told by an educated and reliable gentleman, without prejudice, so to say, to his belief or disbelief in the origin of the illness.

One is apt to smile at any one talking of an animal going up the chimney by the pot chain; frightened animals do curious things. The writer of this, having opened the window in the parlour widely, the door being shut to prevent it going into the house, was trying to drive out a strange cat. There was a lighted fire in the chimney, but the cat, without trying the window, went up the chimney. The fire being damped down and a dustpan put on the top of it, the cat returned to civilisation, and then disappeared through the window.

One other symptom comes from the Black Isle, Ross-shire. H. says that belief in the Evil Eye was very common in his native place, and has a good hold still on people's minds. It was said to do injury to beasts, in many ways, among others that they could be blinded by it. His father had a striking case while living in the Parish of Redcastle. One of his cows died of what was considered a natural trouble, no Evil Eye influence being thought of. He had a quey grazing on the farm of a friend on the opposite side of the Beauly Firth, so he went for her and brought her home by Kessock Ferry, where some people examined her and admired her. She was a dun, and a fine-looking animal. Having reached home the quey was tied in the byre, apparently in good health. They however soon noticed that she had a habit of standing back in her stall to the full extent of the tether rope, and do what they would they could not get her to stand forward. A woman with knowledge of Evil Eye cases was consulted. After examining the beast in the byre by herself she told them the quey was blind, because some one's eye had fallen on her. She recommended the following procedure to cure the animal and find out who had done the injury. She was to be let out and, no one going before her or trying to turn her, allowed to go where she liked. If this were done she said the quey would, of her own accord, go to the house of the person who had made her blind, and that she would go three times round the house bellowing, and then come back to her own byre quite well with recovered sight. This procedure was carried out. She went straight for a neighbour's house, went round it three times, bellowed, and came back quite well and seeing. The reciter added, "Now the woman that could do that and find out things of that kind must have had some power herself, quite as much as the one whose eye had fallen upon the heifer." The reciter of the above is an uneducated man, and superstitious in other ways.

A believer, a native of Knapdale, tells the following. For a considerable time none of her cows had quey calves, but at length she got one, a nice beast, of which she was particularly careful. When it was first let out she went herself to watch it. At that time she had a neighbour who had an ill-will to her, although they were on speaking terms, though without having much to do with each other. While she was watching the calf this neighbour came out of her own house, and putting her hands on each of her sides, stood and gazed for a few seconds at the calf. While she was staring at it the calf gave a 'loup,' rushed as if it were mad through the place, and when, with a deal of difficulty it had been caught and put into the byre, it kept leaping straight up, and seemed as if it could not rest. The person consulted said he could do nothing in the case, and that it was ill from the other woman looking at it. Subsequently she had two more quey calves of which she was very proud and pleased to have them, and as they were grazing in a park near the road, many people admired them. One day the same objectionable neighbour went, and placing her two arms on the dyke, stared at the calves for some time. "I saw her with my own eyes and did not like it, but said nothing." Not long after her daughter came in and said that the white calf was lying dead among the nettles. "On hearing this I trembled, but spoke quite calmly and said, 'Is it?'" On examination, sure enough the calf was dead, and the other was ill also. She consulted a skilled woman, and the remaining calf got better. This reciter added that since then she had lost beasts through the same person's Evil Eye, and is in terror when she sees her coming about the house.

A woman who lived on Loch Awe-side, who was believed to have the Evil Eye, and whose father was also credited with it, was exchanging brood hens with a neighbour. She brought her own hen, and was going to take away the one to be exchanged. In the absence of the mistress, the girl who was keeping the house was going to give the cow a drink, and the woman accompanied her. There was nothing wrong with the cow then, but later in the day the cow's calf died, and the cow herself began to take some kind of fits, and though she lived for a while never got well. When night came the hens were crowing, and next morning two of them were found dead. The hen that had been brought was put on the eggs, but if she was, it was not long that she remained on them. She took to the hills and was never caught, and all this was the consequence of the Evil Eye.

Even more common than injury to cows and calves is the deterioration of milk. Mrs. McL., appealing to her husband for confirmation, told how that in the winter-time she began to churn sometime after dark. Her husband helped her with it, and they had just finished, and she was going to stop and take off the butter, when a young man came in. When he went away she went back to her churn, but not a bit of butter could she get. To gather it she took another turn of churning, but the milk only swelled and went over the churn mouth. The butter was all gone. It was this young man's Evil Eye.

Another nearly similar case to the above, and they could be considerably added to, happened to the mother of the reciter, who was churning, and a woman, supposed to possess an Evil Eye, and also suspected of a measure of witchcraft, coming in, "the butter got scattered into a kind of grainy substance, and do what she would the churner could not get it to gather again."

Horses, of course, are liable to the malign influence of the Evil Eye. — — had a nice white horse which he used to lend on hire to the minister. It was much admired, and one day when it came home a neighbour, who bore the owner no goodwill, came forward and, standing beside the horse, said in Gaelic, "You have got fine limbs;" he then walked away. Shortly afterwards the horse threw itself down on the ground and kicked as if in great pain. It was at first supposed to be an attack of colic, and the son walked it out a little, but so soon as it entered the stable it fell down and was like to die. A woman with skill being consulted, cured the horse and confirmed their suspicion of it being a case of Evil Eye.

Ministers' horses do not escape any more than those of laymen. A Mull woman related the following:—The minister, whose grave you may see there, had a fine horse. His man had it out ploughing, and without previous illness or warning of any kind, it fell down and could not plough another furrow. The minister came to see it.

"A mhinistear, tha an t-each air a chronachadh. Feumaidh mi dhol airson eolas a chronachaidh."

"Eisd, eisd, cha dean thu sin. Tha fios agad nach eil mise a' creidsinn ann a leithid sin."

"Direach falbhaidh sibhse a steach, agus managie mi fein an t-each."

("Minister, the horse is *air a cronachadh*, and I must go for *eolas a chronachaidh*." "Hush, hush, you will not do that; you know that I do not believe the like of that." "Just you go in, and I'll manage the horse myself.")

We may finish the incident which tells how the minister did as was suggested, and how, as soon as he was out of sight, off the lad set for what he considered skilled assistance. Having got it, in less than three hours the horse was quite well and ploughing. When the minister was again looking on, the lad remarked on the rapid recovery from the process used, but the minister was unconvinced.

"Cha'n eil mi dol a thoirt creideas da leithid sin idir."

Thuirt an gille: "Well, *tha mi fein 's an t-each a' creidsinn ann."*

("I am not going to give credence to the like of that at all." The lad replied: "Well, both I and the horse believe in it.")

A like case. "You remember A. B. He had a braw mare; everybody was praising her, and there wasn't the likes of her to be seen about the place. A man who was passing waited to look at her, and praised her for being a splendid beast. But if he did, when she reached home she fell down and would neither rise nor eat."

Mrs. G. said: "One of our horses, a fine beast, was going past the barn when all at once it fell on the ground. They got it into the stable. In a little time it could not move its body, but was tossing its head from side to side and seemed to be in great pain. It was striking its head on the ground so much that we thought it would kill itself."

A case in which the illness had lasted for some time before skilled advice was got, is the following: "D. D.'s father-in-law had a horse unwell and not expected to recover. It was lying in the stable quite stiff, and had neither eaten nor drunk anything for some days."

A farmer who had two fine horses told the reciter to put the saddle on one of them and meet him on his way home from a visit he had to pay.

D. McT., as instructed, saddled the better of the two horses and started to meet his father. He was very careful, leading the horse instead of riding it. He met his father within three miles of home driving in a cart with a neighbour. When they met, his father said, "You have killed that beast. Why did you ride it so hard?" D. told his father, what was the fact, that he had not ridden at all, but walked all the way from home. "Look at the horse," said his father, and the horse was pouring of sweat and trembling. He turned home, but could not keep up with the cart, and only managed to make it crawl back with difficulty. As soon as it was got into the stall, it lay down and commenced kicking as if in great pain. The horse was cured.

A man of whom we have already spoken as injuring animals with his Evil Eye unintentionally, as a reciter tells us, "was at this time threshing with my father. They had no threshing-mill, and did it all with flails. One day my father had been out ploughing, and had the best mare ever they had in the plough. Coming home, he had to pass the barn to go to the stable, and McA., of the Evil Eye, came to the door and looked after the mare. That was enough; before the mare reached the stable door she began to shake and tremble, and it was with great difficulty they managed to get her into the stall. They knew quite well what was the matter."

One other horse case. The reciter says: "One Sunday I was standing there on the little hill at C., and I saw a man coming towards me from Gartachara. I knew the man and waited till he passed. He went down to C. I never thought of anything being wrong, but when I turned down the way the man had come up, what did I find but a beautiful brown horse I had at the time, lying on his belly in the water where the horses used to take their drink. He could not stand on his feet, but I got help, and we managed to get him into the kailyard, where he lay groaning." The horse recovered.

Fowls are said to be affected. A certain woman had been suspected of hindering the butter from coming at a churning. The case was being reported to a collector, when a bystander expressed doubts as to the existence of an Evil Eye. The reciter then said that her own experience had proved the truth of the accusation in the case of this individual. "She was living for a year beside me, and all that year, although I had most beautiful hens, they laid nothing but soft eggs. They would be found in the mornings all scattered here and there on the floor. Indeed I thought they dropped more eggs than was natural. It was only when talking about the hens to another neighbour that it was suggested to me that her Evil Eye was the cause. Then I knew that there would be no use keeping hens while that woman was beside me, so I sold them all. I got clear of her at the end of the year. I never said anything to her about it, for I was afraid."

The reciter of the following said that he was positively certain that the facts were as stated, though it had not occurred to himself. "A certain man once called at a house, and a beautiful brood of chickens were going about on the kitchen floor. He was not right out when a stool fell on them and smothered every one of them. From the kitchen he went to the byre, and saw there a beautiful quey, which he professed to admire very much. He was not long gone when the quey became unwell." The belief was firmly established that the chickens and the quey had been *air an cronachadh*.

A firm believer gives the following:—"One time her mother had a brood of ducks, and every time Mrs. Mac. came in she praised the ducks, but meanwhile one after another was dying, until at last only one remained. One day this one was in the kitchen when Mrs. Mac. came in, and she praised it as usual, but when she was going away she tramped on it and killed it. They were quite sure it was her Evil Eye that had been doing the mischief."

Not only live fowls but even eggs may be injured. B. S., a respectable girl, a domestic servant, able to read and write, and quite reliable, gives this as a sample. She had bought some eggs, and on bringing them home a neighbour woman was in the house and looked at the eggs. She went away, and afterwards some of the eggs were put on to boil. Although left on the fire for the usual time, it was found they were not boiled enough, and were returned to be further boiled. One of them then cracked and sent the hot water in sparks in her face, and the others were so broken that they were of no use. The people in the house attributed the mishap to the woman who had been there when the eggs were brought in.

On considering the whole of these symptoms, the principal thing that strikes one to be urged in excuse of the faith that is in the reciters is that what was wrong came on apparently suddenly, in some cases after a visit from a person already suspected, but as often as not it was the suddenness of the mishap which gave ground to the accusation of some probably entirely innocent passer-by. Unless faith in the Evil Eye were already present, there seems hardly ground for any person with experience of cattle and their ailments to evolve a theory of the existence of any such latent power in the individuals accused. So little critical people became, that everything unexpected was referred to the Evil Eye. As a Kintyre man said, "If anything went wrong with the beef when the winter supply was cured, it was attributed to the Evil Eye of some one or other."

BENEFIT TO THE OWNER OF AN EVIL EYE

Though in many cases involuntary, it has been pointed out that some believe that individuals knowing or professing to know that they have an Evil Eye, from sheer devilry, exercise it to the injury of others, though for no visible benefit to themselves.

A reliable and fairly educated woman, whose father began life as a crofter and died what in that class of life is to be considered as a rich man, a native of South Uist, relates:—There was a woman near her father's house believed to have a very bad eye, and to be able to do mischief with it. Her aunt was very careful as much as possible to keep out of this woman's sight, and if she happened to come about at churning time her aunt would put the churn so that the woman would not see it. She would not sell a pound of butter to her for any consideration. The curious thing was that although that woman could take away the produce from other people's cows, she seemed unable to make any profit of it for herself. It was just her envious and malicious nature that made her take it (the produce) from other people, although it was not going to benefit herself. She was well known by all the people in the district, and they all suspected her of the practice of witchcraft. It was on account of this suspicion, selling butter to her was objected to.

It is not necessary that the desire to possess something should be, as it were, illegitimate or unreasonable to cause damage. Thus M. MacL. was relating how a neighbour's horse had died. "People say that it was blighted by the Evil Eye. One of his sons had his eye *in* it, for he expected to get it for himself, but it took ill. At first they thought it was going to get better, for it was eating its food in the evening, but on the following morning this son went out to the stable when he rose, and found it lying down. When it saw him it got up, gave itself a shake, and fell down dead."

There may be, however, indirect advantages from being credited by your neighbours with having an Evil Eye. Mrs. MacE., a cottar, lived on the farm of L. in one of the inner isles. She was believed to have had the Evil Eye very strongly, and people would do almost anything rather than offend her, so general was the impression that she could injure any person if she wished to do so. The reciter served for some time on a farm that marched with hers, and he says that when Mrs. MacE. came their way she could have almost whatever favour she chose to ask, so much were they afraid of her Evil Eye. He often heard his master remark that he would not incur her displeasure for almost any consideration, in case she might do him injury.

DISADVANTAGE TO THE OWNER OF AN EVIL EYE

If in an indirect way, as above pointed out, some benefits may accrue to one credited with the Evil Eye, it is also said that they may personally suffer serious loss. An old Islay woman who can read Gaelic well, intelligent and full of information, says she knows for certain there are people who possess the Evil Eye. She believes that it is not a matter of choice with them, they cannot help it. Some even do harm to their own cattle. R., who was at one time in Islay, could not go into his own byre but one or other of the cattle would be ill after it. This was so well known that a big dairymaid that he had engaged, a north-country woman, protested against his coming over the byre doorstep. It was because he had such an envious eye that he did so much mischief.

Another reciter tells us of the same farmer that they kept him in the house when his own cattle were being taken in from pasture, in case by admiring them he might be the means of doing them an injury.

Another man in the same island, having got a first-prize animal, said to the herd that he would go out to see it. The herd, fearing evil, tried to dissuade him, but he persisted in going. Shortly afterwards the animal died. His neighbours used to hurry their cattle out of his sight when they saw him coming that way. It was said he could not help it.

D. C. had the Evil Eye very powerfully. On one occasion he went to examine some cattle he had newly bought, and when he looked at them some of them fell down as if they would die. The herd ran across the hill to a hamlet marching with D. C.'s farm and got a bottle of water from a skilled person. When sprinkled on the cattle they at once recovered.

A man in Bowmore went into his own byre one night when his cousin, who lived with him, was milking his cow. He had a nice calf in the byre, and he put his arms round its neck and began to praise it very much. His cousin said to him it was not good to do that. The next morning the calf was found dead, an occurrence credited to his Evil Eye.

A native of Mull avowed her firm belief in the Evil Eye, especially quoting what her mother had told her of a large farmer where she had been brought up who owned a number of cattle, and who had the Evil Eye. "Every time that man went into his own byre the best of his cattle were sure to be unwell afterwards, and they were often dying with him. He could not help it. At last he got a dairymaid who, when she had become acquainted with his peculiarities, would not allow him to go into the byre at all, or near the cows. She turned him back when she would see him coming."

Exactly the same account of another farmer is given by a reciter in Ross-shire in the parish of U— —. She knew him very well by sight, having often seen him at markets, and many times she had heard that he had the Evil Eye, could not help it, and often hurt his own cattle "by thinking too highly of them." This information was corroborated by another, D. McL., who also knew the man by name and sight, having served on a farm in the same district, and he often heard of him hurting his own cattle.

Of course the Evil Eye is as lively in Ireland as on this side of St. George's Channel; but the following experience of a native of county Cork, an educated, reliable woman, the wife of a member of the lower ranks of the Civil Service, while staying in Jura, is interesting. Desiring a drink of water one day she called at a house, the mistress of which met her at the door and invited her to come in to have a drink of milk. When she went in she found a girl churning. After sitting for a minute or two Mrs. M. would have left, but was urged to wait for a little to taste the new butter off the churn on a scone. She sat a while, and the girl continued at the churn, evidently working as hard as she could, perspiring, and yet there were no signs of butter. Mrs. M. innocently remarked, "Dear me, I never thought churning was so difficult." The woman and girl looked at each other, but without speaking. The girl continued churning, until at last her mistress said, "You may put the churn past, you will get no butter off it to-day." Shortly after Mrs. M. left without having tasted the butter, but beyond that thinking nothing of the circumstances. About two months afterwards, while walking in the same direction, she called at the same house. When going in she noticed the girl again at the churn, but making a rush with it to the other end of the house. Mrs. M. observed, "Oh! Mrs. Mac., I hope I am not interfering with your work. I see J. going out of the way."

"She is churning, and is going away with the churn, for the last time you were here she did not get one bit of butter off the churn."

"I am sorry to hear that; I am sure I did nothing to keep the butter from coming."

"I do not know; she got none at any rate, that's all I can say."

Of two women living beside each other in Islay, one was credited with the Evil Eye, and supposed to take away the dairy produce from her neighbours. One year her neighbour for a whole summer was unable to get a bit of butter from her churning. Her suspicion rested strongly on the other. Her account of it was as follows: "I tried everything. They told me to put a horseshoe in the churn, and I did that. Others told me to put salt in it, and I did that, but neither did any good. I scrubbed and scrubbed the churn and the milk dishes, but it was of no use. The milk would only come up with a hissing sound. I was even afraid to use the sour milk in baking scones, for I was sure there was something not right about it. The pig got fat that year, for it was getting the most of the milk. At last I consulted a neighbour, and she told me just what I knew already, that it was a bad woman beside me that was taking away the butter. She advised me not to bother any more, and to keep churning, for the woman would stop her mischief by-and-by, and then the butter would come back as it had gone. I did as she told me, and through time the butter came. I was not speaking about it to any one, for I did not want people to know I believed that she could do so much harm."

A well-educated small farmer's wife, a woman of five-and-thirty, knew a husband and wife who both possessed the Evil Eye. They were quite aware themselves that they did, and could not help it. Passing through a park where several colts were grazing, one of which took their fancy, they expressed their admiration of it. That evening the colt took ill and never recovered.

One would think that a little consideration would have made it clear that with two in the same house equally unfortunate nothing they had could have succeeded with them, and yet there was no account of this couple being in worse circumstances than their neighbours.

It certainly is a curious development, the belief already alluded to of the injurious action of the Evil Eye of the farmer on his own stock. "W. C. was on intimate terms with a neighbouring farmer, whom he visited frequently. It was observed that if at any time he (the farmer) praised an animal, something for certain happened to it afterwards. On one occasion he talked admiringly of the poultry, and shortly after all of them died."

Another reciter said: "In our own time a farmer required to be kept from going among his own cattle, lest by looking on them they should be injured." These cases respectively were in Islay and Harris.

Judging from personal experience of an old friend addicted to prophesying on his first appearance in the morning the sort of weather for the day, the result being, as we of a younger generation all believed, almost invariably wrong, it seems probable that these stories have arisen in connection with men who talked freely, giving opinions based upon hurried observation. Where silence would have left no ground for animadversion the wordy man had his sayings remembered against him, especially when he was wrong, and the good beasts subsequently turned out failures, as the fine days foretold were generally wet.

CONSEQUENCE OF DIRECT PRAISE

The mere expression of admiration should be avoided by those who wish to escape the accusation of the Evil Eye. A youngish woman says, "You have seen my cousin J.'s third boy. He was the finest and nicest looking of all the children. When six months old he was a very pretty child. One day a woman came into the house; the baby was on his mother's arm, and the visitor began to praise the child, and praised it very much. She was hardly away when a man came, and he began to praise the child as the woman had done. After he went away like a shot the baby took ill. They did not know what was the matter with him, or what to do, for he was growing worse. He continued in that way for some days. At last granny said she was sure he had been *air a chronachadh,* and advised the mother to consult a woman who was supposed to have knowledge to cure such cases. J. was not willing to go at first, but granny insisted that it would do no harm at any rate to go and speak to the woman. She went, but did not tell anybody at the time, for of course they would be speaking about it. As soon as she told the woman why she had come, the woman told her that the child had been injured by the Evil Eye, and she described exactly the man and woman who had done the harm, although my cousin had not mentioned man or woman to her. Was it not wonderful how she knew the very ones that had done it?" She cured the child. The above happened in one of the islands.

The following is from Ross-shire (Tarbat): "One of my sisters was blighted by a woman who lived beside them. She was well known for her uncanny ways. The way the thing happened was this: The little girl was tied on an elder sister's back, and they were sent out for a walk. They had not gone far when the woman in question came forward, and putting the shawl back from the child's face said, 'What a pretty little girl! which of them is this?' When the children returned their mother found that the young one was very ill, and on questioning the elder girl, she said that they had met this woman and repeated what she had said. Mother at once suspected what was the matter, sent for the woman, and charged her with having hurt her child. She protested that she had not done the child any injury, but the elder girl spoke up and said, 'Yes, you looked at her and said she was pretty, and did not bless her.' The woman admitted this, and that if she had done any harm to the child she was sorry for it, but it could be sorted if wrong had been done. She operated a charm, and the child was soon as brisk as ever."

A domestic servant relates that a woman who lived in Kil C. had a first-rate cow that was giving a large quantity of milk. One evening when she was milking another woman came into the byre and began praising the cow, and expressing her amazement at the quantity of milk she gave. No more was thought of this, till at next milking the cow did not give so much, and continued to get worse. It became evident that she had been injured by the person who had praised her so much.

A Campbeltown man says, "I am sure I do not know about these things, for I have never seen anything of it myself, but I mind my neighbour over there, D. M., saying to me one day not long ago, that a woman was going past some time before that, and she began to praise one of his cows, saying what a grand udder she had and such fine teats. No doubt the cow was good, he said, and a fine milker, but after that day her milk went from her."

A married woman of about forty-five "believes firmly in the existence of the Evil Eye," and relates as a proof: Mrs. McD., a neighbour, told her lately that she was churning. The butter was actually on the churn when Mrs. B. came in, and looking into the churn began to praise the stuff, and said how well off she was to be getting such beautiful butter. She just stayed a minute or two and then went away. After she was gone the butter scattered on the churn, and do what she would she could not get it to gather again. All she could get was froth, and it continued that way with her for several churnings.

A girl of twenty-four, a domestic servant, a crofter's daughter with a good School Board education, said, "*Cronachadh* is still in it. My mother was churning not long ago at all, and that woman Mrs. C. came in, and looking into the churn said, 'Oh! what a lot of butter!' Well, the butter went off, and though my mother churned and churned she did not get a bit of that churning, nor for a churning or two after that. We believed that the butter had been taken away."

A woman who admits that she is a firm believer in the Evil Eye, tells of the following case within her own knowledge. Two women were living beside each other, and she knew them both personally. Each had a pig, and they were striving whose pig should be fattest. One of them had a cow, the other had not. The one that had the cow was giving her pig lots of milk. It was growing fast and surpassing the other. One day the neighbour came in, and while they were looking at it and saying how well it was thriving, she remarked, "*Cha'n iongantach a mhuc agadsa bhi cho math on is e sin an seorsa biadh tha thu toirt dith.*" ("No wonder your pig is so good, since that is the kind of food you are giving to her.") After a little while the woman left, but was not long gone when the pig took ill, and when it was apparently getting no better they sent to Gortan-na-lag for one living there believed to have knowledge. When he came and saw the pig he said they had been too late in sending for him, and told them at once that it had been *air a cronachadh*, and he showed them who had done the mischief.

A *cailleach*, notorious as having the Evil Eye, was calling in the house of an acquaintance of the reciter, and when she was leaving she praised a fine hen that was in the yard. It was one of her best hens, and the woman praised it very much. That very day what happened but this hen was taken in dead, and the woman declared she could never get out of her mind that it had been a case of Evil Eye blight.

A LOOK DOES IT

The belief in an Evil Eye having arisen, it is perfectly clear that a mere look, quite unaccompanied by any other action, would soon be considered a quite sufficient cause of the mischief such an eye would occasion. A gamekeeper's wife, a "canty body," as she is described, told how some lads on a Sunday, who had watched a mare and foal grazing for some time, were credited with damaging the foal, because shortly after they left it lay kicking on the ground and would not suck.

A horse going up the main street of Bowmore in Islay was looked at by a man passing. A few minutes after it fell and could not rise, till a woman, C. McI., came and did "something to it." The horse got all right, and the woman consulted maintained that it was a case of Evil Eye.

A man now resident in Glasgow was visiting some friends on a farm in one of the inner islands, and a man riding past was observed looking rather attentively at the cows in a field beside the road. He was supposed to have paid particular attention to a cow which, shortly after he had passed, was noticed to be unwell. It was treated as a case of the Evil Eye, and recovered.

These cases occurred with persons not notorious. The following is one in which the woman who affected the cattle was generally believed to have the Evil Eye. The reciter's father was driving four cows from the park one evening, and when passing this woman's house she stood at the door looking at the cows. In a moment off they went as hard as they could run. One of them, a handsome beast that had been bought from a farmer in Gartbreac, when they got them into the byre, was tied to a heavy kitchen grate which was there, but she ran out of the byre with the grate hanging to her neck, and climbed up a peat stack nearly reaching the top of it. From that day they never got any further good of that cow, and were decidedly of opinion that she had been bewitched by the woman.

Not the cattle alone but milk also is influenced by a mere look. We give an instance in the words of the narrator:—

"Bha 'n toradh air a thoirt uam fein an uiridh. Mhaistir sinn gus an robh Raonull agus Donull agus mi fein a ruith leis an fhallus ach ged a leanamaid air fathast cha 'n fhaigheamaid mir ime. 'S an anns an t-sabhal bhios sinn a cruinneachadh a bhainne agus thainig duine 'n rathad latha aig nach eil bo da

chuid fein agus dh'amhairc e air a bhainne 'san t-sabhal: bha sinn a' deanadh dhe gum b'esan a rinn an cron. Bha na cairdean gam' chomhairleachadh gun a bhi leigeil le daoine bhi faicinn a'bhainne ach mi bhi cuimhnicheadh nach eil na h-uile duine cosmhuil rium fein. Well, o'n am sin, tha sinn a toirt fanear nach fhaigh neach sam bith cothrom air dol far am bheil am bainne agus tha sinn a faotainn a nis urrad ime's bu chor air na h-uile maistreadh." ("The butter was taken from myself last year. We churned until Ronald and Donald and myself were running with sweat, but although we had continued at it till now we could not get a bit of butter. It is in the barn that we gather the milk, and a man who has not got a cow of his own came the way one day and he looked on the milk in the barn, and we were making out that it was he who had done the harm. The friends were advising me not to be allowing people to see the milk, but that I should remember that every person is not like myself. Well, from that time we are taking care that nobody will get an opportunity to go where the milk is, and now we are getting as much butter as we ought to get on every churning.")

The Isle of Man, from a Gaelic point of view, may be considered as likely to be much the same as the islands of Argyll, and a lighthouse-keeper, stationed there for some time, tells us he heard a good deal about the Evil Eye, and that belief in it is pretty common. "If a person is seen to look closely at a cow when passing her he is at once suspected, and is likely to be requested by the owner of the beast to take certain steps to prevent injurious consequences."

As we have seen above, the very natural consequence of this belief in a look doing injury leads to the hiding of things liable to harm.

A somewhat amusing story of the effects of a look is from Arran.

"One time M. K. and myself were at a meeting, and there was an old bachelor there who kept looking at us all the time. We noticed it, but did not think much about it until after we went home, but when we got home both of us began to yawn and rift, and could not stop it. We were quite sure that we had been hurt by the 'eye' of the old fellow. M. K. made a drink of salt and water for us, and we took it and that cured us."

Eructation in Arran seems to have a special connection with the Evil Eye and witchcraft. Another reciter remembers quite well a reputed witch going into her mother's house, and not very long after she left her younger sister, a child at the time, became unwell. Her mother at once suspected that the fault lay with the woman who had left, so she sent after her and brought her back. The reputed witch "mixed salt and water, drank it herself, rifted fearfully, and in a little while the child got quite well."

The use of salt as a "preservative" is illustrated in the case of an Arran woman who was a strong believer in and much afraid of the effects of the Evil Eye. She had one cow, and it gave her much discomfort when she saw the cow grazing near the roadside, fearing that some passer-by might "put his eye in her." To keep the milk right, if she gave any to be carried away, or even "to be drunk on the premises," she invariably put salt in it, and that sometimes to excess. The reciter said, "For a while we were getting milk from her for a man staying with us who was seriously annoyed when the milk was more than ordinarily salt, giving vent to his discontent saying, 'Why the deuce does she not let us put saut in oor ain milk?'"

AVOIDING THE LOOK

The following recited by a Mull woman is interesting as showing that smiths and Druids, or their modern representatives, have still some affinity. The reciter told how her mother's cow had taken suddenly ill as her brother Sandy was starting for the smithy. When he arrived there he mentioned the circumstance to the smith. "'And did your mother no send any message to me?' said the smith. Sandy said, 'No, she had sent no message.' 'Well, I think your mother might ken that anything that I could do, I would do for her, and she might have sent for me.' My brother suggested that he had better come away down to see her, so the smith came down and found my mother very vexed about the cow. He said, 'The cow is bad enough, but it might have been one of the family, for the one that could do this could do the other thing just as well, but we'll see what can be done.' Having taken certain steps, he advised her also not to allow any one to see the cow on any account, for three would soon pass, he said, and if she would allow them in to see the cow, the cow would be gone. The three were strong, and she would need to use all her strength to keep them out. He told her that was all he could do just then, but that she must send Sandy over twice to him for a bottle. When he went away she told the children not to tell any one where she was, and she went to the byre to watch the cow. Having got tubs she filled them with stones and placed them against the byre door with spades and everything she could think of to keep the door from being opened. She was not long there when a man passed with a horse and a dog. He came to the kitchen door and asked the children where their mother was, but they did not tell him. He then came to the byre door, lifted the sneck, and when it did not yield tried to force it open with all his might, saying, '*A Cheit nic Iain, am bheil thu ann sud?*' ('Kate, John's daughter, are you there?') My mother knew his voice as that of a near neighbour, and answered: '*Tha Iain, tha a' mhart gu bochd agus tha i na laidh cul an doruis 's cha 'n urrainn dhuit tighinn a steach.*' ('Yes, John, the cow is unwell, and she is lying behind the door and you cannot get in.') My mother had to tell the lie, or he would force the door open. The man went away, and these were the three that the smith had said would come the way—the man and the horse and the dog.

And it was that man that had done the harm to the cow, but it was found out in time and the cow got better, but it was that very year my two brothers died, and nobody knows whether he had anything to do with their death or no."

We include this under Evil Eye, because there is no statement of any accusation of witchcraft against the "man," or for the matter of that "of the horse or the dog."

In another case, in which a certain George T., by his devices, cured a cow of which he had said it was "bitten, wounded" (*teum*), he asked if there had been a man with a black head praising the cow. When he was told that they had no knowledge of such a thing, "Well," said he, "it is a man with a black head that has injured your cow with the Evil Eye, but be under no anxiety, the cow is all right now." He asked my mother if she had shown to any person the whole of the butter that came off the churn. My mother said that she was not showing (was not in the custom of showing) the butter to any one. "That is right, Flora. For all you have ever seen, although you would not keep but as much as the size of an egg, be sure that you do not let the whole of the butter be seen by anybody."

An Islay farmer's daughter remembers a certain woman who was supposed to possess an Evil Eye, and who paid them occasional visits. So terrified were they lest she should interfere with their butter, that whenever they saw her coming while they were churning, they would throw a cloth over the churn and put it out of sight until the woman left.

From Stratherrick, Ross-shire, a reciter said, "When she heard so much talk about cattle being injured by the Evil Eye, and the substance taken away, she became afraid of this, and especially when churning disliked anybody to come where the churn was, so much so that she used to do the churning in an out-of-the-way corner of the house."

It is evidently not so easy to protect a horse or a cow from a glance of an Evil Eye, but a lady tells how that, visiting at a farmhouse, she saw the old cook, who had been long in the farmer's service, running in great excitement to gather in a brood of young ducklings that were running about the yard. Being a frequent visitor and intimately acquainted with the cook, she asked her what was wrong, and why she was hurrying the ducklings at that hour of the day. "Oh," said the cook, "Mr. A. is coming up the road, and last time he was here I had a beautiful brood of ducklings, and his eye took them and every one of them died, so I am putting these out of sight in case he should look at them."

According to one authority the influence of an Evil Eye does not cease at once with the absence of the possessor. "W. G. lived for some time on a certain farm; she was supposed to be possessed of the Evil Eye, and on one occasion it was particularly noticed that certain animals she had praised died. When removed from the farm, the farmer met with a succession of misfortunes which were credited to W. G."

CONVERSION TO BELIEF IN EVIL EYE

We have already seen a case, in which a woman on her own showing demonstrates that it was the influence of others which caused her to believe in the power of the Evil Eye; but conviction has in some cases been carried to the minds of men as a result of experience. A man taking a valuable horse from the west coast of Kintyre to Tarbert was, after leaving Musadale, offered a considerable sum for it. He said he would not, could not sell the beast, and though the offer was raised to sixty pounds, he still refused and went on his way. Before he reached Tayinloan the horse fell dead on the road. The owner of the horse, considered to be a religious man, after this incident could not be shaken in his belief in the Evil Eye.

In another case, a woman having got from her mother a hen, a first-rate layer, an acquaintance came in and the conversation turned upon the excellence of the bird, frankly acknowledged by the owner, who added her own quota of praise. The visitor was no time gone when the hen "clapped her wings, fell down, and died." Mrs. G. declared that it has been her firm belief ever since that it was a case of *cronachadh*.

GIVING AWAY MILK DANGEROUS

All have heard of the belief in the power of witches to acquire for themselves, among other things, the milk and butter of their neighbours. This apparently requires some deliberate act of magic, "drawing the tether," as they say in the north of Ireland, or even milking the pot chain, as reported in the Highlands. In only one case, as reported, was this danger ascribed to the owner of an Evil Eye, and the writer is still of opinion that his lady friend, who said, "If an evil-disposed person who possesses an Evil Eye gets a little milk from another, he or she will be able to operate through that to injure all the milk that remains, and even the cows," had not differentiated in her own mind the "Evil Eye" from "witchcraft." We will repeat the incident.

A suspected woman, living near, one time asked her servant if she could get a little milk daily, her own cow giving none at the time. The servant girl told the lady that the woman was asking milk, and then added, "I will not give it her." Her mistress said, "Oh, you may give it; she needs it, and you can spare it quite well." The girl said it was not that, but showed that she was afraid of the woman getting what she asked, and thus taking their milk from them and perhaps injuring the cow. Her mistress said there was no fear of that, and the girl yielded, adding, "I know what I'll do." What she did was to put pinches of salt and of sugar in the milk the woman was to get that evening, and to take the first mouthful (*bolgam*) of it herself. This, according to prevalent ideas in the district, would hinder the receiver of the milk having any power to do harm for the remainder of that season. This performance seems a common precaution in cases where milk is given to suspected persons.

SCIENCE VERSUS EOLAS

It will be easily understood that to a believer in the Evil Eye mere modern science, as met with in daily life, in doctors, and veterinary surgeons, is of small account. A well-educated lady, a friend of the writer, advised a neighbour whose cow was ill to send for the vet. The answer was: "*Cha'n eil vet a chum feum sam bith, oir 'san a tha bho air a cronachadh. 'S e rud is fearr eolas fhaotainn air a son.*" ("A vet is no use whatever, because the cow is *air a cronachadh*; the best thing is to get *eolas* for it.)"

In that case they didn't even send for the "vet." In the following instance a certain preliminary confidence seems to have been shown in medical men. The reciter gives this as a very clear case of Evil Eye. A child had fallen sick; two doctors were attending it, but it was getting worse. The parents, having done all that they could think of, requested the aid of a woman who was known to deal with *eolas a chronachaidh*. The woman went to see the child, and what she did the reciter did not know, but, "sure enough, she soon cured the child and told its parents that it had been *air a cronachadh*." This may have been "sure enough" for those immediately interested, others may be permitted to doubt.

In these cases common sense has generally the minister on its side. In a case already quoted, in which the mother's milk was supposed to have been turned into water in her system by the Tiree woman, her mother was sent for. This old lady's granddaughter tells us, "When my grandmother came she suggested that a decent man who was living near them, who was used to work with *eolas* where people or beasts had been *air an cronachadh*, should be called in, but she said they would need to go to him secretly, for he had promised the minister that he would not make any more *eolas*. My father and mother agreed, but my mother requested my grandmother to go to the man, because she did not know how to go about it. My grandmother went and spoke to the man's wife first. The wife said, 'I am sure he will do what he can for John (the child's father), but he has promised the minister that he would not make any more of that; but come and speak to him yourself.' My grandmother spoke to the man, who said that he had promised to the minister that he would not do any more of these things. He could not go to her, but she might come back to him again the following day. This was a Wednesday, and there were only two days of the week on which he could make *eolas*—these were Thursdays and Sundays. When she went back the following day, he had not got his cure ready yet, he said, but would have it on Sunday. He told her that her daughter would not have so much milk as she had at first, but would have enough to bring up the child. On Sunday he had the thing ready as he had promised, and he made it twice for her afterwards. That is, he made it three times. He correctly described the whole appearance of the woman who had taken the milk away, although nobody had ever mentioned about the Tiree *cailleach* to him. My mother had plenty of milk after that."

We can scarcely wonder at the minister objecting to this magical practitioner when we consider the nature and the time of his performance. An old Islay man says that when he was a young man he was very intimate with a woman who had knowledge of the curing of toothache (*eolas deide*). She was a relative of his own, and many a time she offered to teach him the words she used. She could teach them to a male, not to a female. He was young at the time, and did not like to learn them, for some people were saying that it was a sort of witchcraft (*buideachas*), but it was not that, for the words were all good words. They were taught by the Saviour, who taught them first to His mother. Our reciter went on to say that this toothache cure is of no use, and need not be tried, in any case beyond a first or second attack. It is hard to make it succeed even in the case of a second attack, and beyond that it can have no effect whatever. Neither will it do in a case where the sufferer has his tooth taken out.

These latter confessions were doubtless memories of the instructions of the teacher. Our old friend did not repeat the formula, but it has appeared elsewhere. [6]

The "some" who said that *eolas* was a sort of witchcraft seem undoubtedly to be right, unless, of course, we admit that their action is based on a scientific understanding. The Evil Eye itself is unconscious, and therefore a natural phenomenon like measles or hay fever, but its cure is a good deal like that employed for hay fever in many cases, more empirical than scientific.

[6] "Gaelic Incantations, with Translations," W. Mackenzie, p. 55 *et seq.*

We are lucky in being able to give in his own words medical science as expounded by a Gaelic-speaking tailor, a simple-minded man of about seven-and-thirty, a man who can read and can work, but with no special affection for either. He belongs to one of the inner islands:—

"Tha Eolas nathrach ann, agus tha Eolas deide ann. Tha Eolas sul, agus Eolas greim, agus Eolas chronachaidh ann. Eolas gach ni, 'na aite fein. Ma lotar neach le nathair, faigheadh e Eolas nathrach: agus 'nuair bhios an deide air duine faigheadh e Eolas deide; agus mar sin leis gach ni eile. Is aithne dhomh fhein da neo tri, a fhuair leigheas airson lot nathrach. Tha na facail th' aca airson Eolais greim air an toirt as an Tiomnadh nuadh, pios an so, agus pios an sin; agus iad sin air an sgriobhadh air paipear, agus am paipear sin air fhuaigheal air an taobh a steach de chot' an duine air an robh an greim. Cuiridh so an greim air falbh. B'aithne dhomh fhein duine a dh' fheuch so, agus rinn e feum dha. Ach feumaidh duine bhi cinnteach gum bu na facail ceart aige. Agus tha na facail airson eolas deide air an cuir air paiper, agus am paiper air fhuaigheal an taobh a stigh de aodach duin' air a cheart doigh. Ach ma tha na fiaclan air falbh, cha dean e math sam bith, ach ma tha iad slan fathast, ni e feum, agus cha tig an deide air ais tuille.

"Chuala mi iomadh uair na facail th' aca airson Eolas sul; ach bheir mi dhuibh na chrunas an t-iomlan—ni a thug Mathair da Mac gus olc a chumail air falbh, bho'n bhainne agus bho'n chuinneag. So na briatharan:—

''Nuair a ni thu toiseachadh.

Cuir dorlach math salainn ann.

Cuir bun 'us barr an neonain ann.

Cuir mionach roin, 'us gearr fheidh ann.

Buain slat de'n chaoran a nall o aodann Eallasaid.

Snathain dearg le snuim teann

Air a chuir mu cheann a' chratachan.

'S ged a thigeadh buidseach Hendry.

Cheannsaicheadh am balach i.'

Tha sibh a faicinn, bha 'm buidseach Hendry anns a Bhioball. B' ise' m buidseach bu laidire bha beo riomh; ach nam faigheadh neach sambith na nithe sin uile, agus an cuir gu feum, cha b' urrainn dhise neo do bhuidseach sam bith eile a chron a dheanadh. Chunnaic mi fein an snathain dearg air clann, gus olc a chumail bhuapa."

("There is serpent knowledge (serpent bite) and toothache knowledge. There is eye knowledge and stitch (gripes) knowledge and hurt knowledge (by Evil Eye or Witchcraft). Knowledge of each thing in its own place. If any person is wounded by a serpent let him get serpent knowledge, and when a man has toothache let him get toothache knowledge, and so with every other thing. I myself know two or three who got a cure for serpent bites. The words they have for curing stitch (gripes) are taken from the New Testament, a bit here and a bit there, and these written upon paper, and that paper sewn in the inside of the coat of the person who had the stitch. This will put the stitch away. I knew a man that tried this, and it was of use to him. But one must be sure that he has got the right words. And the words for toothache knowledge are put on paper, and the paper sewn inside a person's clothes in the same manner. But if the teeth are gone it will do no good, but if they are still whole it will do good, and the toothache will not return any more.

"I have often heard the words they have for eye knowledge, but I will give you what crowns the whole, the thing a Mother gave to her Son to keep evil away from the milk and from the churn. Here are the words:—

> 'When you make a beginning
> Put a good handful of salt in it.
> Put root and flower of the daisy in it.
> Put the entrails of a seal and a hare in it.
> Cut a wand of rowan over from the face of Ellasaid.
> A red thread with a tight knot
> Put on the head of the churn staff.
> And should the witch Hendry (of Endor) come.
> The boy would conquer her.'

"You see the witch Hendry was in the Bible. She was the strongest witch that ever lived, but if any person would get all these things and use them, she, or any other witch, could not do him injury. I have myself seen the red thread on children to keep evil from them.")

The above is undoubtedly sheer witchcraft, white witchcraft, if you like. It is not then surprising that the evidence is not in favour of these *eolas* professors being held in much social esteem. A native of Harris, talking of one of them, said: "Notwithstanding the wide reputation the man had, and the many who went to seek advice, he was not held in high esteem, and this part of his occupation was not admired although so many took advantage of his services." The reciter himself spoke of him as *bodach granda* (nasty old man).

A Gaelic-speaking minister gave the following information. It refers to Arran. He knew several old women who professed *eolas a chronachaidh*, but he did not hold a high opinion of them. One case, however, he remembers especially in this connection. A lad was taken suddenly ill, supposed to be a case of *cronachadh*. An old woman, who was respected in the district, came to see him, and going above him in the bed, made motions with her hands over him and on her own person, repeating an incantation of some length at the same time. The lad recovered. The reciter admits the fact, but does not incline to accept the *eolas* performance as having caused the recovery.

A reciter in Mull was telling before her mother of the operations of a *cailleach* of this sort, when the mother added, she herself had spoken with the woman, she was a decent body, and assured her that there was nothing whatever wrong in what she did for the cure of cattle when hurt by the Evil Eye. The words used were good, and she repeated them, but she added that a great deal depended upon the person who applied for *eolas*, and that, unless such a person believed that a cure would be effectual, there was little use in what she herself could do, and no use at all in the contents of the bottle which she supplied. It might just as well be thrown out on the roadside.

HURTER AND HEALER

A farmer's wife, an old woman, but smart and intelligent, and showing no failure of memory, expressed the following opinion:—

The power to do injury to beast or person, and the power to cure such an injury appeared to have been given to different classes of people. Those who did injury were supposed to be malevolent, and of course held in bad repute, while the curers were looked upon as for the good of people and to be respected. What the one did was called *cronachadh*, and what the other did *beannachadh* (blessing).

To another, an Islay lady, the remark was made that *cronachadh* was a strange thing. In answer she said: "Yes, but *beannachadh* was quite as strange." "What is that?" "*Fiosrachadh or eolas*." (Knowledge the result of inquiry, and knowledge apparently arrived at in any way, say by revelation.)

That is one side of the picture. We see the other in the following:—

"There was a lad at service at one time with Malcolm here beside us. He was one of the T's. He was in the habit of coming to this house, and my father said to myself, I should not have too much to do with him, for that there was something bad in him. It was maintained that his father had *eolas*, and people would be going to him when a beast or person was unwell, but those that have the one thing, the knowledge of healing, it is usual for them to have the other thing, knowledge to cause injury also." The reciter believed that this lad deliberately did them an injury, and after recounting the particulars said, "My father advised us not to show any anger to the lad for fear he might do something worse to us, if he were to know that we were angry. 'That is the way the like of these people have. If they do harm to a person and he shows anger they will do him more harm.'"

A domestic servant, speaking of an old woman that she knew very well, said: "She was known as Mairi Siath (Mary of sprains?) and was looked upon as one who had a great deal of secret power by which she could do both harm and good. People were afraid to offend her, and would give her almost anything she would ask rather than offend her." The said Mary, having been consulted about unsuccessful churning, "brought back the butter every bit that should have been on the churn from the time it had been taken away, and there was so much that the mistress was afraid to use it in the house, for she said it could not have come in a right way. She gave it away, and after that they always got butter on the churn."

There is no doubt that the girl who repeated this believed what she was telling as of her own knowledge. The only explanation that occurs to one is that the milk, having been for some reason poor for a time from bad feeding or some such thing, the food having become better and richer, the milk was thereby improved to such an extent as to give the appearance, especially in comparison with the small yield before, of a somewhat supernatural supply.

The same belief in the power of hurting and healing being united in one person has been already mentioned in connection with an Arran shepherd.

One other case as reported was that of an Islay farmer who, on one occasion riding along the road, passed a man ploughing with a pair of horses. Shortly thereafter the horses lay down, having become to all appearance unwell. A messenger was immediately despatched after the farmer, who, hearing what had happened, returned, and at any rate got the credit of curing the animals.

TRANSMISSION OF EOLAS

It has already been mentioned how a woman who possessed a toothache cure was willing to impart the necessary formula (incantation) to a "relative" who was a male, but could not do it to a female. That case was in Islay.

The following information from Skye shows the belief that *eolas* is imparted in the same way and under like circumstances there. This Skye woman was believed to have the Evil Eye, and to have the power of taking away the produce (*an toradh*) from other's cows. When she was on her deathbed, and when she came very near her end, she said to those about her that she was anxious to see her husband. He happened at that particular time to be out looking after something, and they sent for him, but all the time till he came in she kept crying for him, and urging that she wished to see him. When he came in she requested that all the others should withdraw, and when they had done so she said to her husband to shut the door that there might be nobody there but themselves alone. What took place between them there nobody ever knew, but one thing people firmly believed, that was that she gave the skill that she had to her husband, for after that he could take away the *toradh* from other people's cows, and did take it away too.

However, authorities do not always agree as to changing the sex in the transmission of this magic.

A native of Harris, a woman of about forty, has no English, and can neither read nor write. When asked as to her experiences, and if she had ever seen a thread tied round a child's neck to preserve it from the effects of the Evil Eye, she said: "I did see it; wasn't there one on my own child? and that was for A. McE.'s Evil Eye. She has an Evil Eye (*Droch shuil*), and one day she came into the house and began to praise the child greatly. She was only a short time gone when the child began to vomit. 'O Kate,' said I to my sister, 'my child is *air a cronachadh* with the Evil Eye of that woman.' 'If that is all that is wrong, we won't be long putting it right,' said Kate, and she took a red thread, and when she had said the word, she tied the string on the child's neck, and there was no time till it was quite well." She was asked whether Kate had the words, and she replied, "Oh yes, my mother had them and she taught them to Kate."

The general trend of belief is that the hereditary transmission of *eolas* is from father to daughter, and from mother to son. A reciter said: "A woman still lives in the neighbourhood, said to have obtained her *eolas* secret from her father. She is often requisitioned, and her skill to cure fully believed in."

Another said: "You know A. McE. His mother had *eolas a chronachaidh*, and he said that she left the secret with him before she died." These were "unprovoked" statements of the reciters, and in the latter case the interest of the story was in pointing out the method taken to determine whose Evil Eye had affected a sick horse. The owner was told to watch the colour of the hair of the first woman that passed the house, which would be the same as that of the person wanted. The result was given in the following terms, "Now she is blaming Mrs. MacD."

In all these cases we see that the *eolas* was kept in the family, or at least believed to be so. The deathbed scene of the wife and husband may be a most uncharitable suggestion of heathenism, but the recital was made in good faith.

The witch doctor sometimes apparently requires assistance. A horse being taken ill while ploughing, supposed to be hurt by the Evil Eye, the farmer refused to have anything to do with these irregular practices. The horse died. Not long after a second took ill, and as the ploughman, the reciter, said, "We were all about it saying it could be cured." At last the master said if there was any person who could do it they might try it, it would do no harm at any rate. There was a man there that had *eolas*, and he took another man out with him, and they made the *eolas* outside. They did nothing to the horse, but while they were out making the *eolas* the horse got up, shook itself, and was better at once.

In Arran, as elsewhere, *cronachadh* seems to be regarded as hereditary. One reciter said of a man at Loch Ranza that it did not matter what he would look at, his look would *cronach* it. A lad from another part of the island went to ask a daughter of this man to marry him, and when the nearest neighbour heard of his courtship she became exceedingly angry, and protested against any of that man's daughters being brought there "to *cronaich* everything about the place."

FORMS OF INCANTATION

For specimens of these incantations the reader should refer to "Gaelic Incantations, with Translations," W. Mackenzie, Inverness, 1895; and to "Carmina Gadelica," A. Carmichael, Edinburgh, 1900. Above we have already given one as recited, but they are hard to get, there being many reasons why the user is shy of repeating them. One thing is certain, that a complete performance of any of these rites requires the repetition of "words," as they say, of some sort. In far the majority of cases, the words are what are called "good" words, having a sanction of Christianity about them, being generally invocations of the Trinity and of Mary. As a native of Morven said, describing a cure in which water is used at a certain stage, "The person making the *eolas* kept saying good words." Another woman from Mull, describing a cure done by herself, said: "I remember a child I cured myself with good words that I have. It was very ill, and nearly gone when I took it and placed it in my bosom and cured it. I said the words over it, but after curing it I was very much exhausted until I got a cup of tea, and then I felt myself getting better." When requested to repeat the words, she affirmed that they were all good words, and that it was in the name of the Trinity she did it; but she went over the words in such a low voice, and with so indistinct a pronunciation and so fast, that the collector found it quite impossible to follow.

The writer was mentioning these circumstances to a lady visiting him who gave the following example, which aptly illustrates how the performance of some ceremony can form a foundation for belief in their beneficial activity. Her sister's child of three weeks old was lying exceedingly ill and two medical men were in attendance, one having been called in as a consultant.

They told my visitor themselves that the child could not live. The family are Scotch, but this occurred in the neighbourhood of London. The monthly nurse suggested and urged baptism. The clergyman was sent for, and while going through the ceremony the child, who had been lying motionless, made some slight movement. Within two days that child had recovered, and is at the time of writing this as many years old as it was then weeks. The consultant subsequently expressed his dissatisfaction with the infant for having belied his prognosis.

In a case from Mull a servant, having been sent for a means of cure to a woman supposed to have skill, she found her in bed. She sat up, took the bottle containing water which had been sent for, put the mouth of it to her own mouth, and began to say some words over it. The words were spoken in a low tone, but so far as was recognised they were all "good" words.

In the case of a sick horse already quoted, the man who saw it went at once for G. T., then herding in the neighbourhood. The description of the interview is as follows: "When I reached him he said, 'Peter, you need not tell me your business here.' I said, 'No.' We went together to a little stream, and he said that I might now tell him what had brought me. When I told him, he asked me if I had tobacco. They do nothing without pay; not money, but tobacco and things like that. I knew he would ask for it, and I had it with me, and when I gave it him he asked if I had a bottle. I had a good notion of every turn he had, and so had taken a bottle with me, and when I gave it to him he turned his back to me and began lifting the water and saying the words. There was not a bad word in all he said, no, no. He said to me when he gave me the bottle and told me how to use it, 'Your horse will be all right, Peter, as soon as you use it.'" His statement came true.

Things are not, however, always reported as of such an innocent and Christian character. A collector happened to be present at a conversation between two believers in the Evil Eye. One of them said, "Those who are working at such as that, applying *eolas*, are not helped but by the 'bad one,' for if it were that they were doing good they would not need to be hiding themselves when they would be at it. P. McL., a decent man, said his cow was injured, and sent for A. T. The cow was in a little hut, and when A. went in where the cow was P. put his ear to a little window that was in the wall, and he said, that when he heard such language as A. had, he would never again send for her should every cow he would have be unwell. She put her cap under her two knees—she was bare-headed and with her knees bare, but kneeling on her cap apparently—and she prayed to the vile one. ('*Ghuidh i ris an fhear mhosach.*') B. said, 'Was that the time she said that my father's brother injured the cow?' That was the very time. You were living beside P. then."

FORM OF PAYMENT

"The labourer is worthy of his hire." A case has been already given where the reciter said that nothing was done without pay, but not of money. We must not generalise in that way. A native of Tiree says, speaking of his experience in the cure of a horse of his father's, "All these *eolas* folk must get a piece of silver. It may be a shilling or two shillings. This they say makes the cure more certain, and they cannot promise a cure without it. The lad took with him a two-shilling piece and went to an *eolas* man who lived five miles away."

Apparently the silver is given in the form of money as the most convenient medium, though there is good reason for the supposition that the whiteness of silver makes it specially appropriate as a medium of remuneration.

The instance in which the child that was ill is described as if singing "do re do," the woman who cured it received from the father tea and sugar which he had taken with him when he went to consult her; but she said to "my man" (it was the mother who recited the incident) "that she was not wanting anything and would do it for us for nothing, but that he would need to come back with white silver. I sent him back with a sixpence to give her."

An innkeeper, a well-read, shrewd woman of about five-and-forty, tells of a case with which she was well acquainted in which a near neighbour consulted an old man, wanting him to bring back her butter. "She said that she would pay him if he would bring it back to her." He said that he did not want payment, but at the same time he could not bring it back unless he were paid in silver for doing so; that being so, he would require to take something from her, as otherwise the cure would not be successful. So she gave him the silver and soon had all the butter that she lost."

Another reciter having been accustomed to do the churning in his father's house, after his father's death, his stepmother sent for him because she herself could not get any butter from the churn. He did his best, but was unsuccessful. Having had a horse cured by *eolas*, he suggested that the same man should be consulted. The man arrived, and the case was explained, the woman stating, "*Feuch gun toir sibh dhachaidh an toradh oir tha e air falbh.*"

("Try if you can bring back the due produce, for it is gone.") "I'll do that," he said, and he did it by his *eolas*; there was plenty butter on the churn. It cost the woman a crown, but if it did, that was better than that the butter should be lost.

A woman who prepared a bottle for a sick cow charged the man who consulted her "two shillings for the bottle, and when she took the money she poured a little water on it and spat on it." She might, one would think, with advantage have changed the order of her proceedings.

A sick bull which the veterinary surgeon had given up was referred to an *eolas* woman, the principal argument being that her assistance "would only cost a shilling." She ordered a bucket of water to be thrown over the animal, and it recovered.

A Mull woman tells how her grandmother when newly married, after having reared calves, could only get butter of such an ugly colour that nobody would eat it, and it was used for greasing wool before carding. She was asked by a neighbour for a bowl of butter one day, and accused of greed for refusing it while she had eight cows. She explained the position, and was then advised to consult an old man, the neighbour adding that she would be coming back in a fortnight, when there would be plenty of butter to give her. The results of the consultation were fairly successful, though the *eolas* man explained that she would not for that year have so much butter as she should have, but that she should consider herself lucky that her cattle had not died. The reciter then said that her grandmother gave the man "plenty for his trouble, but did not grudge it." When the old woman called on her way back she said, "Well, you can give me the butter now." To which her friend replied, "Yes, I am thankful to you that I can." And she gave her a good bowl of butter.

In the above case payment seems to have been in kind. A native of Ardnamurchan tells of a neighbour of her mother's who had a number of cows and lost the due product of the whole of them. Her mother's people were sitting down to dinner when a beggar woman came and asked, "*An sibhse a' bhoirionnach a chaill an toradh?*" ("Are you the woman who has lost the milk and butter?") "My mother was very fond of her neighbour, and thinking she might find out on her behalf how the milk might be got back, she answered that she was. The beggar woman said, '*Ma bheir sibh dhomh lan meise de mhin bheir mise air ais dhuibh e.*' ('If you will give me a (wooden) dishful of meal I will bring it back to you.') My mother said that she would give her all that was on the table if she would bring it back, and then ran to the neighbour's house to tell what she had heard. They returned together and told the beggar woman whose cows really had been ill." They are said to have been cured. Here also the payment was promised in kind.

A native of Harris tells us of an old man in Stornoway much consulted, who "would undertake for so much money to bring milk and butter back."

An Islay man gives us "*ni a chunnaic mise mi fein*" ("a thing I saw my own self"). This was the cure of his father's cow. A certain George T. "came the way" "*b'e duine corr bha ann an Deorsa so, aig an robh moran sgil mu'n chronachaidh.*" ("This George was a decent man, he had much skill about *cronachadh.*") The cure is described, and the reciter continued: "*Cha b'e duine bha' n an Deorsa a ghabhadh rud sam bith: 'se sin cha ghabhadh e pris airson a sheirbhis ann a leithid so do ni.*" ("George was not a man that would take anything for his service in such a thing as this.") "And my mother said to him, 'Will you take a cup of tea, George?' 'It is I that will,' he said, for he had been about the cow a long time. When they were taking the tea they were keeping an eye on the cow now and again. She took a long time that she did not bend down her head, but at last she gave a shake to herself, and George said to my mother, 'Your cow is right, woman.' In a little while she gave the next shake, and again the third shake, and with that she was as well as she had ever been."

THE NECESSITY OF FAITH

A native of Lewis who professed disbelief in the Evil Eye, though she knew numbers who did believe, was advised when her cow was ill to send for a skilled woman. She refused. A woman who was in the habit of assisting when they were busy, being told she might do as she liked, went to the *eolas* woman. When our reciter, Mrs. McN., looked into the byre shortly afterwards she found the servant girl and the occasional assistant hiding a bottle. "I asked them what they had in the bottle. The woman answered that she had just gone to K. McI. for *eolas*, and that that was what was in the bottle. They had put it in the cow's ears and over her back in the name of the Trinity, and the woman remarked that if it would not do good it would do no harm at any rate. I told them again that I did not believe in it at all, and as it turned out I did not need to believe it, for the cow died not long after. But if I did not believe the woman did, and so did the person who had made the *eolas*, and they maintained that it was because I did not believe in it that it failed to cure the cow, for it is believed the success of *eolas a chronachaidh* in its attempts to cure depends much upon whether it is believed in or not."

Compare this with the statement of another reciter, who on hearing of a case of cure said, "When I was herding, one of the cows was *air a cronachadh*, but the people did not believe in *eolas*, and if it had not been that some of the neighbours went to A. T. the cow was dead."

In another case in which the owner of the sick cow said that there was many a thing that might happen to a beast, and that she did not believe that the cow had been hurt by the Evil Eye. A friend persisted in her opinion that it was the Evil Eye, and when the reciter's mother refused to send for *eolas*, the woman went off herself and came back with a bottle which she sprinkled on the cow, and in less than an hour the cow was eating as well as ever, and before the water had been put on her she was groaning and would neither eat nor move. The probability is, of course, that if no success had followed the application of the remedy, want of faith on the part of the owner might have been urged as a reason for failure.

PREVENTING EVIL BY BLESSING

A young man who could read and write, the son of a decidedly superstitious father, said if any one were praising another person's beast, and danger was suspected, because praising by one that has an Evil Eye is dangerous, if the owners say "God bless it" that would prevent any mischief happening.

A native of Bernera (Harris) mentioned as among the ordinary precautions effective against the Evil Eye a person blessing himself. While another mentioned the keeping of ripe rowans (*caorain dearg*) beside him, or regularly blessing himself and his belongings, as sufficient to prevent any injury coming to him from the Evil Eye or Witchcraft. This blessing seems to have been done in quite a formal way. An old believer who can read Gaelic remembers having seen cattle blessed for the purpose of keeping away evil, and when she was young it was common in the district where she was brought up, when neighbours visited one another, for the visitor on entering the house to bless both the house and the people living in it. In this connection she told the following story: "There was at one time living in the Harris district of Islay a gentleman trained in the knowledge of the 'Black Art' (*Sgoil Dhubh*). He visited the Laird of Balinaby and took from every cow on his estate its due produce (*toradh*). He and the Laird passed this cow, and the visitor remarked: 'You have a witch on the estate.' 'No,' said the Laird. 'Oh yes, there is no doubt of it.' 'Well, if there is, it is without my knowledge.' 'To whom does that cow belong?' 'To a widow that lives in the house over there.' 'Well, she must be a witch, for I can take the produce from every cow on the place except that one, but I am beat with her.'"

Balinaby called at the woman's house and asked her what she did to protect her cow. "I do nothing," said the woman. "You must do something, for I find that the *toradh* can be taken from every cow on the farm but yours." "Well," said she, "I am a God-fearing woman, and am thankful to have the cow. Every morning I pray that she may be preserved, and when I go to milk her I bless myself and the cow. That is all I do." This is evidently traditional, and is quoted merely as an evidence of belief in the protection granted to those who audibly place themselves under the protection of the Deity.

It is a curious fact that Balinaby (the Abbot's Town), bulks very largely in the supernatural folklore of Islay.

A native of Tarbat, Ross-shire, already quoted as telling of a child taken ill because the visitor had not blessed it, details that visitor's action for the cure of the child, when taxed with the dereliction, as follows. "She asked a bowl from my mother and a silver coin, which she got. She put the coin in the bowl, and going to the bedside where the child was lying, sprinkled the water on the child's face, and wet her lips and the palms of both her hands. While doing this she blessed the child, repeated some words over it, and in a little while the bairn was quite well and as brisk as ever."

The materials used in this cure will be considered in more detail, but the blessing was evidently an important part of it to repair a neglect in the first instance.

An old lady in Arran remembers being told of an older generation who, desiring not to injure their own or another's beast lest there should be evil in their eye unknown to themselves, always took the precaution of blessing the animal before looking at it. The words they used were "*Gum beannaicheadh Dia am beathach*" ("That God may bless the beast"), or "*Gum beannaicheadh Dia an ni air am bheil mo shuil ag amhairc.*" ("May God bless the thing my eye is regarding.")

PREVENTING BY DISPRAISING

The expression of a blessing seems to be merely a preventative, which of course is better than curative, if we accept the general proverb. Another preventative, when the expression of praise seems likely to be hurtful, is to miscall the animal spoken of. A man ploughing, who thought very well of his horses, said to his master on seeing another he knew approaching, "Here comes — —, and he will ruin both the horses if he can, for he has the Evil Eye." His master said, "I'll tell you what you will do, and if you do it he can do the horses no harm. When he begins to praise either or both just begin to run them down, and be sure you say as much against them as he shall say for them." He of the Evil Eye came up, and commencing with "What a fine pair of horses you have," went on to enumerate their good points. The servant objected that they looked better than they were, that their looks were the best of them, and for every point in their favour the other mentioned, the lad said something to counterbalance it. The other began to show signs of impatience, and went on his way not very well pleased with the way his opinions of the horses had been disputed. "Well done, you have saved the horses," said his master. "Did I do it right?" said the lad. "Yes, indeed, you could not have said more than you have said."

A native of Campbeltown is the authority for the following. Mrs. M'F. from Knapdale resided in Glasgow for some time after her marriage. She was standing at the mouth of the close one day with her first child in her arms when a little woman whom she had never seen before, and never saw again, as far as she knows, came across the street, and looking at the child began to praise it for its beauty. Mrs. M'F. had not the presence of mind to praise it above what the other woman said, nor to miscall it. Had she done either it would have prevented mischief. As it was, the child began to cry as soon as the little woman went away. It continued crying for a day and a half, and never was right afterwards. The child died. Mrs. M'F. was quite certain it had been injured by the eye of the little woman.

PREVENTING BY ROWAN AND JUNIPER

Every one knows of the value of the rowan tree as a preventative of witchcraft. It is equally effective apparently against the Evil Eye. It is scarcely worth while dilating on this, but it would not do to neglect it. A resident in the Chanonry had a near neighbour terribly suspicious of interference with her cow. She would never allow a cow away from her own ground until she had first tied a sprig of rowan to its tail.

A native of Kintyre, the opposite side of the country, connects this observance with May Eve, on which occasion it was common to tie a sprig of rowan to the cattle's tails. Above we have mentioned rowan berries as equally efficacious with a blessing. The rowan is tied to churns as well as to cows' tails. Another reciter mentions a case in which, along with a bottle, a professor of *eolas* "went to the back of his house, taking a thin slice of juniper wood (*iubhar beinne*), which he instructed was to be put between the wood of the churn and one of its hoops."

One cannot help speculating as to what may have caused the use of these plants. We have a hint from the Chanonry that the rowan tree was attached when the cow left her own ground. Now cows leave their owners' ground solely when sent to the bull. In connection with the *iubhar*, attention is called to the curious, incomprehensible shinty formula in which the word iubhar occurs:—

Ciod an caman? (What shinty-club?)

Caman iubhair (Shinty-club of yew).

Ciod an t-iubhar? (What yew?)

Iubhar athair (Yew of air),

of which another reciter gave the slightly altered pronunciation, *iubhar athar* (father's yew). [7]

A native of the Lewis says it was pretty common to protect cows from evil influences by the use of a charmed *burrach* (cow fetter). The *burrach* was made of different things, and when a cow calved it was fixed on her hind legs.

The *burrachs* the writer has seen were made of hair, possibly they may have made them upon occasion of some tough wood.

Note that it was in calving that the charmed *burrach* was of advantage, and thus the observances for the protection of the cattle are solely connected with their increase.

[7] "Games of Argyle," pp. 33, 34.

PREVENTING BY HORSE NAILS AND SHOES

An Arran reciter said: "I was one time staying with a friend here, and I noticed that a horse nail was tied round the churn. I mentioned nothing about it till one day when washing the churn I said, 'I suppose I may take this off,' but would she let me, though she did not tell me why it had been put on, but I soon found that out for myself."

Another authority mentions not the nail but the whole shoe. "The produce of the churn may be effectually protected from the Evil Eye by nailing the shoe of a colt or of an ass to the bottom of the churn. Where this is done there are not on earth that can do it harm, and many people always took care not to expose their churn without a shoe of either a colt or an ass nailed to it."

PREVENTING BY A SMALL GIFT

A well-informed woman, an innkeeper, said that in cases where a person possessed of the Evil Eye admired anything belonging to another, no injury could follow if some little present were given to the suspected person on leaving.

Another, the daughter of a farmer, an office-bearer in the Church, in the same island, gave the same information, but quoting an older authority. Beside her father's house was a woman who firmly believed in the Evil Eye, and the power of preventing it by this gift. The house commanded a view of the road, so that, for the most part, an old woman suspected who lived in the neighbourhood could generally be seen approaching. The woman, to whom the latter was a special object of suspicion, never failed to advise our reciter's people of the visitor's advent. Her advice was invariably given earnestly and in the same form: "*A ghraidh thoir ni eigin dhi, cha'n eil odds cho beag no cho suarach a bhios e, ach thoir ni eigin dhi agus an sin cha'n urrainn i do chron a dheanamh.*" ("Dear, give her something, no odds how little or how trifling, but give her something, and then she cannot do you an injury.")

In the case of churning the small present naturally takes the form of a drink of milk to be given to any one suspected of the Evil Eye, and so a reciter said that one should always, for safety's sake, give a visitor a drink of milk, and stated further that the beneficial effect was added to if the one who gives it first take a little of it herself before handing it to the stranger. As an illustrative incident the reciter told how Black Colin of Balinaby when out hunting happened to go to Balimony at the milking time. Not one of them offered him a drink of milk, "*Ach coma leat*" (But all the same) the following morning when the girls went to milk the cows not a drop of milk could they get, while the cows kept running and roaring as if they were mad. At once the man of Balimony, concluding that the mischief had been done by Black Colin, saddled a horse, rode to Balinaby and took all the milk from the Balinaby cows, transferring it to his own. When Colin saw this he wrote to Balimony to this effect: "*Leig leamsa agus leigidh mise leatsa*" (equivalent to "Let a be for let a be"). The reciter added that the milk was properly distributed thereafter, and that the incident was one of Black Art.

To a student of the old Bardic Irish stories the continual mention of those who are recommended for their liberality to the poetic class simply shows how they used their office for their own advantage. The tricks of the non-producers continue the same now as they were in the days of Cairbre. A poor Bodach passed the house of the manager of a detached farm. He asked if he could get a drink. The manager's wife, who was churning at the time, left her churn and gave him a drink of water. The Bodach took his drink and went away, the woman went back to her churn, but let her churn ever so much not a bit of butter could she get. The milk became merely froth, and swelled up so that she filled all her spare dishes. That churning was no good, nor the next, nor many succeeding ones, till she was afraid to look at her churn. So things were when who should appear but the same old man with the same request. The manager himself being in, translated the request liberally and gave him plenty both to eat and drink. After resting a little the old man rose to go away, and thanking them for their hospitality, added, "If a poor man ask for a drink, do not give him a drink of water." The significant tone suggested to the manager to ask him for advice as to bringing back the butter, offering him any reasonable reward and putting a piece of money into his hand. This he said he would soon do, and told him to tell his wife to clean her dishes and put a piece of money in the churn and churn the next day. The story goes on to say that every scrap that had been lost was got back in one churning.

As the story is told the product of each churning must have been but a small matter, but there can be little doubt that this, if not a Bardic praise of hospitality, is a beggar's one, and the story of course no better than an *ursgeul*. The reciter added a comment of her own: "*Anns na laithean sin cha bhiodh daoine a beannachadh an cuid, agus le sin bha e furasda gu leor an cronachadh.*" ("In those days people were not in the habit of blessing their effects, and so it was an easy matter to do them harm.") No doubt those were the days before the existence of a Free Church, but it is doubtful if there was much less expression of blessings then than in the present.

A PREVENTATIVE BY BURNING CLOTHING

Allusion has already been made, on an Islay authority, to the efficacy of burning a piece of the clothing to avert injury from any one bringing bad news. A Tiree reciter gives the same information a little more fully, and says it protects against witchcraft or the Evil Eye. "If any woman comes into a house who is suspected, those of the house should try to get a small piece of some article of her clothing, without letting her know that they have got it, and throw it on the fire; that will prevent her from taking anything away with her or leave any mischief when she goes away. If they cannot manage to get a bit of her own clothing, a good plan is, when she is leaving, to burn a rag of some kind of cloth in the fire and throw it after her as she goes."

1 Corinthians, iii. 15. "If any man's work shall be burnt, he shall suffer loss: but he himself shall be saved; yet so as by fire."

PREVENTION BY SPITTING

A native of Ross-shire and a minister gives the following information. When he was living in K. a woman there had a child of about nine months old. Another woman came in, and looking at the child on its mother's arm, remarked, "*Tha balach boidheach priseil agad an sin.*" ("You have a pretty, dear boy there.") Without more ado the mother turned the child's face to her and began to spit in it as hard as she could to prevent any bad effect from the other woman's Evil Eye. The reciter said he has, in several places, heard of this being done with the view of preventing harm, and he has often heard a person in the Isle of Skye say "*Fliuch do shuil*" ("Wet your eye") when any person praised any of his cattle. The idea was that this would put away the chance of mischief.

A native of Mull describes the practice as common there, particularly as a preventative of injury to young children. Spit on your finger and rub an eye of the child to be protected with the moistened finger. This was called *fliuch an t-suil* (eye wet), and was commonly practised and believed by many to be a sufficient protection.

A farmer's daughter, whose people have been for generations in the same place in Islay, tells how she was scandalised by this practice. "We had a web of cloth to sew for the boys, and the tailor we took in had the name of the Evil Eye. One day he was sitting on the table sewing, and my brother came into the kitchen to wash himself. He was but a boy at the time, and stripped to his waist. C. B. began to say that his skin was very white, and he was looking very well. '*Fliuch do shuil, 's na cronaich mi,*' ars H. ('Wet your eye, and do not blight me,' said H.) 'They will be saying, that if a body will say that when any one who has an Evil Eye is praising them, the Evil Eye can do them no injury.' Well, when H. said that, my mother did not know where she was standing, she was so much ashamed. You see the man had the name; if it had not been for that she would not have cared much."

But the performance of the full ceremony is still in use, and it is interesting to be able to give the personal experience of my energetic co-worker, to whom I am under so much obligation.

"A native of the Long Island was complimented by me (E. M. K.) recently on the style of her dress, and the smart appearance it gave her, when, to my surprise and amusement, stepping forward and wetting the point of her finger by putting it on her tongue, she placed the finger on my right eye, saying: '*Fliuch do shuil eagal gum bi mi air mo ghonadh.*' ('Wet your eye for fear that I may be wounded.') She did this very good-naturedly, and explained that when one is the subject of what he may suspect to be envious praise, either in respect of person or clothing, he may protect himself from consequences that might result from the Evil Eye, by performing this ceremony on the one who has done the praising."

It would appear that this practice is comparable with the quenching of a cinder in water—by wetting, the fire of the eye may be supposed to be extinguished beneficially for the one on whom it might have an evil influence.

PREVENTING BY CHURNING

It is specially difficult to distinguish between the Evil Eye and witchcraft in the case of loss of the due produce of cattle—butter, cream, &c. Certain preventatives are good for both. When any one is churning and a visitor enters to whom any suspicion is attached of the power of interfering with the butter, any such power can be taken from her by getting her to do a spell of the churning. A woman, a strong believer in witchcraft and the Evil Eye, invariably if she happens to go into a house where churning is going on, takes the churn staff and gives a pull at the churn, believing, by this means, that she frees herself from suspicion if the churning go wrong. This woman, though a professed believer in witchcraft and the Evil Eye, neither professes practising it nor has ever been suspected by others.

An Excise officer in Islay kept some cattle. The servant was churning, but though there was an appearance of butter, it could not be brought to anything. The mistress of the house wondered what had come over the milk, and a neighbour said that a woman who lived in the neighbourhood, credited with the Evil Eye, had been in, and added, the best plan was to send for her and get her to take a spell at the churn, which would neutralise any bad influence she might have exerted. Acting on this advice, the woman was sent for, and on coming was requested to give a turn at the churn. She did not seem to be very willing, but no further remark being made, she took the churn staff and churned for a while, and the butter was got all right.

Another woman who was present when this was told doubted it being in anybody's power to do harm in that way, whereupon the reciter declared that she believed it to be quite true and had experienced it with the same woman, and then detailed how she had caused the fowls to drop soft-shelled eggs, already quoted.

A domestic servant, speaking of this churning difficulty, said that when she went into houses where they were churning they would not mind her. "Many a time," she added, "they have asked me to give them help with the churn." She apparently had not appreciated the reason of her assistance being asked.

The explanation suggested for this procedure is, that if one does not want the churning to be successful they will not do anything to assist it; and, *vice versâ*, if they do give their help it is considered as evidence of their desire to bring it to a successful termination.

PREVENTION BY PECULIARITY IN CLOTHES

When speaking of the liability of nice-looking, well-dressed children suffering injury, the prevention by turning an article of clothing outside in was mentioned. The authorities in these cases are from Harris and from Islay. To show further the extent of this belief, a Ross-shire man says a thing he has often seen done for the prevention of evil influences was to turn a child's coat or other garment wrong side out, because: "It is believed that a witch is rendered powerless in respect of any person who happens at the time when they might be injuriously affected to be wearing any article of clothing wrong side out."

Another preventative in connection with clothing also comes from Harris. When a dress is put on for the first time a small burning peat or burning stick is waved over it, inside and out, and this is believed to be an efficient protection of the wearer from an attack by the Evil Eye. This is evidently the purification by fire already alluded to.

Attracting the Evil Eye by a piece of cloth also appears in the following from a farmer and office-bearer in the church, a man of about seventy, but an undoubted believer in what we may call superstitions. Where he was brought up a rag was put in a *bruchag* (cranny) of the wall at the head of every milk cow in the byre as a protection against the Evil Eye.

TAR AS PREVENTATIVE

The application of hot pitch to open wounds in ancient surgery is a well-known fact. It may have acted as an antiseptic, and like its congener tar applied for skin eruptions, may have so got into popular use as a preventative of evil. In the island of Islay tar was well known as an application against the Evil Eye, but its use seems to have been restricted to Beltane night, May Eve. One of our reciters, a man now of about fifty, when herding cattle as a boy remembers how all the time he was on the farm of C. at a fixed hour on *Oidhche Bhealtuinn* he went to the byre with the farmer and his son. They took with them a small pot of tar and a bit of stick, little larger than an egg-spoon. Our reciter held the dish while the son took hold of the ears of each of the cattle in turn and the old man put a little tar into each ear with the stick. If any words were spoken the boy did not hear them.

Another old man, a man of eighty, can neither read nor write, without any English, adds to the putting it in the ears that it was also put on the noses of the cattle for the purpose of "preventing injuries from the Evil Eye."

Another, a woman of about fifty-five, says her father was regular in the habit of putting tar on the horns of his cows on May Eve to protect the beasts from the Evil Eye.

A fourth reciter says he has often seen it put on the horns and ears, and also rowan berries tied to the cows' tails on the same occasion, and adds that this was usually accompanied with the repeating of some good words to protect the beasts from being hurt with the Evil Eye.

The germicide powers of tar products seem to have been further reaching, and even more highly appreciated in those days than they are now.

NICKING THE EAR

The ears, we now see, played a prominent part in the treatment of *cronachadh*, and we learn on the authority of a minister how that in the case of a quey supposed to be affected by the Evil Eye, the owner loosed it from its stall, cut a slit in its ear, repeating some incantation the while.

From a man of about fifty-five, a joiner, we have confirmation of this. He remembers of a beast dying where he lived when he was a boy, and of seeing the woman to whom the animal belonged and another *cailleach* sitting over the dead beast cutting a piece out of its ear. They kept the piece they cut. On asking why the women were handling the dead animal, he was told that the piece cut from its ear would prevent an Evil Eye affecting the rest of the cattle.

Weak or unhealthy eyes are in popular belief cured by piercing the ear (and wearing earrings).

URINE AS PREVENTATIVE

The detergent, and let us say with all gravity, the cleansing power of stale urine, is well known, and it is hardly to be wondered at when we find this used to clear away, as it were, evil influences.

"There was at one time a farmer in Gruinart who used regularly to sprinkle his cows when putting them out with the contents of the chamber pot. This was with the view of protecting them against witchcraft, and I have done that myself."

Our informant for this was a woman of about sixty. This is supported by another reciter in Islay, who said it was done in the morning.

Two other reciters tell that it was done in spring, or the early part of summer, when they were put out on the grass "for the first time that season." The sprinkling was done with a broom from the chamber pot as the cattle were passing out of the byre.

What was good for cows was also considered good for horses; they also got their share of attention. Finally, in this particular, an intelligent crofter's wife who can read, and is of about seventy years of age, informs us that it was customary to collect the bedroom slops for a day or two before the birth of a child. So soon as the child was born, to prevent any mischief from *cronachadh*, the house was sprinkled both outside and in. She saw this done in her mother's house.

The remark that this sprinkling was done when the cattle were first turned out, and of a statement that it was common among farmers to have the services of a man believed to have *colas* to notch the ears of cattle on May Eve against witchcraft, have to be taken together, May Day being supposed to be a specially active moment for the witch sisterhood. Two reciters mention this sprinkling with "salt" and "urine" in connection with each other. That they were looked upon as having somewhat the same action there can be no doubt, whatever analogy drawn between the two may have existed in the mind of the reciter. One of the two reciters gave an instance which, though undoubtedly unperceived by the narrator, throws a sidelight upon the ideas connected with it. The mother of our reciter consulted an *eolas* man for the bettering of defective churning. He gave her a bottle, directing her to hold it in her hand all the way on her journey home, and on no account to let it touch the ground. When she got home she was to sprinkle some of it on the cow and the outside of the churn, and round about it. On her way home she rested for a minute, and forgetting about the instructions, put down the bottle. Sprinkling the cow did no good, and the scientist was again consulted. *"Leig thu leis fheum a chall,"* ars S. ("You allowed it to lose its usefulness," said S.) *"Rinn i gair bheag ag'radh gun do leig i sios e car mionaid."* ("She smiled, saying that she had let it down for a minute.") *"Chaill thu e mata."* ("You have lost it, then.") Now comes the incident mentioned his retiring to the back of the house and giving his consulter the slip of *iubhar-beinne* (juniper), the flavouring matter of gin, the most diuretic of stimulants.

Putting all this together, it is not difficult to see why part at least of the magic fluid would lose its effect if it touched the ground, the place it most naturally reaches, if we accept Burt's statement, in Highland houses, and even in a recognised house of entertainment. "But I had like to have forgot a Mischance that happened to me the next Morning, for rising early, and getting out of my Box pretty hastily, I unluckily set my Foot in the Chamber-pot, a Hole in the Ground by the Bed-side, which was made to serve for that Use in case of Occasion." [8] When the next bottle reached the house and not the ground, the effect was quite satisfactory. The reciter of this openly professed belief in the whole story, even to the recovery of the missing butter.

Many will rise up in arms against my suggestion that the water to be used, and which was used, and which is called water, was in many cases and in its origin urine. In the Clonmel witch-burning case in Ireland in 1895, Mrs. Cleary, the victim, had "water" thrown over her, fetched by her cousin from an adjoining room. This was brought three or four times, and the process of sprinkling lasted at intervals over a period of ten or twenty minutes. This water, according to the *Cork Examiner* and other reports, was called "a certain noxious fluid." According to accounts given by Leitrim people, the most effective way of disenchanting folk was to throw over them a concoction of strong urine and hens' excrement. Compare with this the Arran man's charm against the Evil Eye. [9]

[8] Burt's "Letters from the North of Scotland," vol. ii. p. 65.

[9] See "Folk-Lore," vol. vi. p. 378.

The general protective power of stale urine is curiously illustrated in the following from a Mackay. The reciter said when he was young it was a general custom throughout the Reay country to have a tub of stale wash placed at the door cheek with a little stick always standing in it. The stick was preferably, if it could be got, of blackthorn—sloe. The object of this was that visitors might stir up the contents of the tub before going into the house, a process intended to protect the house and its inmates from being injured by any bad luck or misfortune, or evil of any kind, that otherwise might accompany the visitor. To comply with this condition was reckoned a sufficient passport for any caller, and no matter who he was, or on what business he had come, he was expected to do the stirring before crossing the threshold. The reciter said that he had done it himself regularly in his youth.

The conclusion arrived at that the water supplied in some cases, and in any case what ought to be supplied by the practitioner of *eolas*, was diluted urine, seems to get important endorsation from the following on the authority of John Kerr, LLD., late her Majesty's Inspector of Schools:—

"A man had a child suffering from water in the head, and carried him on his back in a blanket from Lochcarron to Lochbroom and back—over a hundred and twenty miles—to see a man who professed to cure such ailments. He got a bottle of water, a spoonful of which was to be given several times a day. The doctor found the water absolutely putrid." [10]

[10] "Memories Grave and Gay," John Kerr, LLD., p. 323.

Dr. Kerr having this from a medical man, one is inclined to fancy that the description of the dose is given in a method corresponding to an ordinary prescription; spoonful doses remind one of the regular practitioner. The diagnosis 'hydrocephalus' is the doctor's; the man consulted was not a curer of water in the head, but of the results of witchcraft or the Evil Eye. This, there can scarcely be any doubt of, or that that also was the father's idea of the cause of the child's illness—it had been *air a chronachadh*. Here the important point is the putridity of the water. If it had been pure water it might have been vapid enough, but we may be certain that no licensed practitioner would have said that the fluid was absolutely putrid without sufficient cause. The diagnosis is that its putridity was occasioned by containing a greater or less quantity of stale urine.

A BURNT OFFERING

The following is vouched for by an intelligent and educated young lady resident in Orkney, though as it is from a non-Gaelic island it takes us to a different people from those we have been occupied with.

In one of the islands there a farmer was losing his cattle one after another. The general opinion, in which the farmer himself concurred, was that the fatality arose from some person's Evil Eye having lighted on the stock. It was also considered, as the best means of putting an end to this, to burn one of the remaining animals alive. This was done, and report has it that everything went well enough after that. This case seems sufficiently notorious, though no more exact information has been procured; but the Evil Eye is strongly believed in in Orkney, and our informant herself knew a man who, on finding things "going back" with him, as they say, confidently attributed his unprosperity to some one having put his Evil Eye in his effects. Many of his neighbours, knowing the circumstances, were of the same opinion as himself.

CHARMS. (STRING)

"No Christian shall attach short strings to the neck of women or of animals, even if you see this practised by churchmen, and they should tell you that this custom is a pious one." Such was the pronouncement of St. Eloi of the Abbey of Luxeuil, in the seventh century, the successor of Columban, as reported by St. Ouen (Audoenus) in the "Nos Origines." [11]

[11] *Les Influences Celtiques*, by Charles Roessler, p. 59.

So far we seem to have seen that the damage done by the Evil Eye was a malign dispensation of Providence, for which the owner was only to blame to the same extent that one is to blame for a natural defect, but the processes of cure being the result of science, so to say, *eolas, fios*, are in reality magic processes. One of the most common of the preventive charms is something to be worn by the person to be protected, and one reciter, an elder in the church, assures us that he knows a family every member of which wears such a charm suspended round the neck.

This must have been something of the nature of an *ubag*, a thing which takes the form generally of what, referring to American Indians, is spoken of as a "medicine bag," but which the Dictionaries translate as a charm—an incantation. A much more common protective is the *sreang a chronachaidh*, or *snathainn cronachaidh* (string or thread of hurting).

The form that this took differed considerably. One reciter says it was made of different colours of yarn, an incantation was said over it while being made, and when finished it was tied round the child's neck. She has often seen these in use, and did not think that it mattered anything what colours were used, provided that there were different colours in it.

Another reciter says that the strings before being put on were soaked in something, but does not mention if they were coloured, while two others mention the fact, of their personal knowledge, that the threads they had seen worn were red.

In one of the last cases the thread had been put on to cure a child supposed to be already suffering. In the other, while the thread was used as a protection, the reciter mentioned as a curative where something had gone wrong with the first child of a marriage, especially if there was any suspicion of *cronachadh*, that some article of clothing which had been worn by the mother on the first night of marriage, was put round the child three times, and "There are some," said he, "who take the precaution to do this as a preventative even where no injury is suspected as having already taken place."

One of our reciters quotes the following verse of a song as an authority for the efficacy of the red thread:—

> "Snathainn dearg, is snuim air,
>
> Bi sud air ceann a' chrandachan;
>
> Ged thigeadh Buidseach Henderson,
>
> Cheannsaicheadh Ailean e."
>
> ("A red thread, and a knot on it,
>
> That will be on the top of the churn staff,
>
> Though Henderson the *witch* should come,
>
> Allan would subdue him.")

There can be no doubt that it is our old acquaintance the Witch of Endor who here again appears as Henderson.

The following is the account given by a man suspected of the Evil Eye, who watched secretly through a chink in the door the performance by a professor of *eolas* who was supposed to have inherited his skill from his deceased wife. The Evil Eye doctor went direct to the churn, which stood very much on the middle of the floor, and walked round about it several times, "six or seven," says D. McF. Then taking a ball of yarn from his pocket he wound it round about the churn-staff, putting a good many turns on it. This done, he gave the staff two or three turns as hard as he could, as if churning. He then came out, but in a short time returned, and D., securing his point of observation, saw him take the yarn off the churn-staff and wind it round the churn itself. Again he gave a few turns at churning, and finally left. The reciter was uncertain whether or not any benefit accrued to that churning itself.

The following method in the case of a lad on the one hand, and of a cow on the other, demonstrates pretty fully the method of using the red yarn in Harris. The skilled woman, having assured a sick lad that she knew what was wrong, and that it could soon be put right, having requested all present, except of course the patient, to leave the room, procured a ball of *three-ply* yarn and wound it round the points of her thumb, middle finger, and ring finger of her left hand, holding the thread between the thumb and mid-finger of the right hand. Having done this she took a small piece of burning stick and passed it three times through the circle formed by the thread on her fingers. She then put a knot on the cord, bringing it close to her mouth, and repeating a lengthy incantation commencing, "*Ni mi an obair so*" ("I do this work"), in which were references to the "eye." The knot having been put on and the incantation finished she took the yarn off her finger, and commencing at the crown of the head, she rubbed him with it in a round and round way all over. At this stage there was a knock at the door to which the performer replied: "You are there, I know you," and without opening the door, put the knot into the fire, saying, "*An galar 's caslainnte chuirinn air mulach an teine.*" ("The disease and the illness I would put on the top of the fire.") She repeated this three times, and on the third occasion, instead of putting the thread in the fire (it would appear from this that she had made three knots, and not one as the description would lead us to suppose) she tied it round the lad's neck. The thread is always tied, said the reciter, where it will not be seen, but it must be on the skin. Some wear such a thread as a precaution against the Evil Eye. It was explained that the knock at the door was done by the individual causing the illness.

The following is the information as to the conduct of the operation in the case of a cow, and our reciter saw this herself. The *eolas* operator first asked for yarn in which alum had been used in the dyeing. Our informant explained that it was necessary that any yarn to be used should have had alum applied to it, and as alum is always used in dyeing red (as a mordant), red is very generally what is taken on such occasions. Having got the little ball of red yarn, the thread was wound round the fingers as above described, and here we learn categorically that the forefinger must not be allowed to touch the yarn throughout the performance. There was no burning stick here used, but having taken the yarn off her finger, a knot was put on the thread, the knot put to her lips, and an incantation alluding to the eye muttered with it in that position. This winding, muttering, and knot-tying was gone through altogether three times with equal care. Commencing then with one of the horns of the animal, she rubbed the cow down with a circular motion all over till she came to the other horn, and then tied the first knot on the cow's tail, taking care to have it out of sight, the three knots being tied one after the other to the under hairs of the cow's tail. When the cow showed signs of improvement the first knot was taken off and burned with the words used above. The same performance being carried through with the second knot, but the third knot was allowed to remain on the cow's tail. This woman refused to impart the incantation formula to any but a member of her own family, and it is believed that the greater the admiration of the operator for the person affected the more effectual the cure.

A native of South Uist said that while different methods were employed to cure the Evil Eye, the most common, so far as she could judge, was the

Snaithnean (thread). This was so well known that when the Evil Eye was suspected in the case of an animal, *faigheamaid snaithnean dhi* (*dha*) (get a thread to it), and away they would go to an *eolas* person. The snaithnean is simply a red woollen thread four or five inches long. The giver of it says some good words over it, hands it to the messenger with instructions to go straight home and tie the thread round the animal's tail till it recovers. In more important cases the professor may deem it advisable to fasten the string on himself. The reciter, though not admitting belief in the charm as such, has seen this done several times with good effect.

The above statement was thoroughly corroborated by another from the same locality, who "has often seen the red thread on beasts' tails." She spoke of the injury as *gonadh* (wounded).

An Islay woman remembers as a girl, in the case of a cow of her mother's, where a string was put on the cow that was ill, but as they were all turned out of the byre she does not know what else was done.

Another reciter in the same island, in the case of one of his own horses, which was said to have been injured by the evil eyes of drovers, had it cured by a woollen thread being tied round its tail.

Before leaving the red thread, a reciter in Islay, whose aunt lived next to a professor, said that when this woman was consulted in cases of Evil Eye, she took a bottle containing a red thread and water, and for the purpose of discovering the cause of the animals' illness she closed her eyes and repeated an incantation. This done she would open her eyes, and the first living creature bearing any burden or weight, that weight, whatever it might be, she maintained she saw pressing upon the animal. A case in point is the following. Having gone through her performance when consulted about a sick cow, on lifting up her eyes they rested on a man carrying a horse collar. She told the owner of the cow that the spirit of that man with the collar was pressing on the animal, and would continue so until the water which was in the bottle, over which she had repeated the incantation, was sprinkled on her. If after that the cow shivered all over she would not get better, but if she merely shook her ears she would be all right. The people about, the reciter added, had great confidence in this woman's professions.

Another reciter said that when a child was not thriving a red thread was tied round its neck and allowed to remain on night and day. He has seen this where he knew both the child and its parents very intimately.

It must not, however, be supposed that red thread alone was used. Another Argyllshire reciter has seen on Hallowe'en different colours of worsted thread tied on cattle as a prophylactic.

The mother of the child, in which the symptom of injury by the Evil Eye was its seeming to sing "do re do," gives the following account of the thread tied on it which cured it. His father went to an *eolas* woman and told her his business. She took some lint that she had ready to be put on the spindle and twisted a little bit into a thread. It must always be green lint that is used for these threads. She made a string that would go three times round his neck, and getting the man's knife she wound the thread round the steel, and handing it to him ordered him to hold it in his hand all the way home, and not to open his hand or speak to anybody till he would reach home. He was then to put the string three times round the child's neck, and as he was getting better one string at a time was to be taken off and thrown into the fire. This was all done as directed, the "humming" stopped, and the child got quite well.

A native of Strontian gave the following as his own experience of the use of a green thread. When a boy he had a "fallen" uvula, and was sent to a woman who was said to be able to "lift" it. She took him into a corner of the house and commenced manipulating the outside of his throat and below his chin, speaking all the time as if to herself. At all events he could not follow what she said, though he heard the words *Sheumais, Eoin, 's Pheadair* (James', John's, and Peter's) frequently. Having done this some time, she tied a green thread about his neck and sent him away, saying it would be all right. Mr. McD. added the remark that he had nothing to give the operator, though it is essential that something pass from your hand into theirs. A reason for this was given by a native of Fort William, that "unless the curer got something for putting the trouble away the trouble would go on him- (her) self."

A curer of cases of Evil Eye in the neighbourhood of Ballachulish, though her method of treatment was not wholly known to the reciter, part of it consisted in giving water and two threads (three articles), one black and one white. The threads were to be twisted in a prescribed manner round the person or animal affected, and if the threads showed any tendency to knot, it was taken as a sure sign that it was a case of the Evil Eye, *i.e.* apparently if they formed *eyes* on the thread.

Ligatures other than thread were used. A native of Easdale tells how his grandaunt used to tell him of a relative who lived with her father. He was a farmer, and losing his cattle, and believing that they were being affected by the Evil Eye, took his courage in both hands and marched off to consult Campbell of Skipness, distinguished for his skill in such cases. Having told his errand, Campbell took him into the barn and, excluding all light, made the people—that is, the Evil Eye people—pass before him, and he recognised them quite well. Campbell then gave him a *gisreag* (charm) made of a straw rope, and requested him to take it home with him and throw it into the fire as soon as he reached his destination. This was to protect him against further injury. The man burned the *gisreag* on reaching home, and from that day his cattle throve quite well.

Another reciter remembers that her brother having gone to consult a professor of *eolas* on account of serious losses to his stock, while he was away a new horse, bought to take the place of one that had died, was taken ill between the plough chains. Well does she remember, on her brother's return, seeing him take the tether with which it had been tied, and waving it three times over the horse, it got up at once, took the food offered it, and was soon all right.

From Tomintoul, Banffshire, we hear of one who had a wide reputation for skill in these matters, who was said to perform his charms by means of a bridle that was in his possession. We have no further particulars, but it is not impossible that the bridle was a rope one.

There has been mentioned the case of a young horse where the result of the Evil Eye was to make it pour of sweat and tremble. Having got it back into the stable, a recognised practitioner of *eolas* was sent for. Among his questions was one whether the lad who was leading it had, or had not, met any one on the road. He then asked for the halter which had been on the horse, and it having been brought him he said one or two words which nobody present seemed able to catch, after which, waving the halter three times over the animal, he said, "Rise and eat." At once the horse got on its feet, began to eat, and was cured. McA., the *eolas* man, now said it was a case of *cronachadh*, and offered to tell who had done it. They assured him they did not wish to know. But the reciter made the naïve remark that "he knew already, for he knew who had met him on the road."

UISGE A' CHRONACHAIDH (WATER OF INJURY)

We have already mentioned, as one of the results of the Evil Eye, a bad attack of yawning. Here is the account of the sufferer's cure in the words of the reciter. "*Chuir iad airson sean-mhathair Sheumais Ruaidh so agus nur a thainig ise rinn i eolas le beagan uisge agus facailean, agus cha robh a chaileag tiota an deigh sin gus an robh i cho mhath 's bha i riamh. Dh'innis a bhean a leighis i ra mathair gur h-ann air a cronachadh a bha i.*" ("They sent for this Red James' grandmother, and when she came she made science with a little water and words, and it was but a short time till the girl was as well as ever she was. The woman that cured her told her mother that she had been injured by *cronachadh*.")

The water used here was what has been called in Arran at any rate "*uisge a' chronachaidh.*"

One other account of this Evil Eye water we will give in the words of the reciter, an old man speaking of his daughter:" '*Nuair a bha 'm bas ag'oibrich rithe thainig i dhachaidh an so agus bha e soilleir gum b'ann air a cronachadh a bha i. Nis chuala mi fhein daoine ag radh nam biodh neach air a chronachadh agus nam biodh bonn airgeid air a chuir ann am bowl uisge a bhiodh air a thoirt a tobar o'n taobh deas, nan leanadh an t-airgiod ri grunnd a' bhowl, nuair a dhoirte an t-uisge dheth, gun cuireadh an t-uisge sin an cronachadh air falbh nam biodh e air a chrathadh air a' neach a bha fo'n chronachadh. Well, chaidh mi fhein gu tobar a bha ris an taobh deas de'n tigh agam agus chuir mi bonn se sgillinn an an lan bowl-de'n uisge ach nuair a thaomadh an t-uisge dheth, cha do lean am bonn ris a bhowl. Ach co dhiu chrath mi 'n t-uisge oirre ach ged a chrath cha d'rinn e feum sam bi, 's cha deachaidh i riomh ni b'fhearr. Ach bha daoine ag radh nan robh an t-airgiod air leantuinn ris a' bhowl gun deannadh an t-uisge an cronachadh a thoirt air falbh.*" ("When death was working with her she came home here, and it was clear that she had been blighted. I myself heard people saying if any one were blighted and a coin put into a bowl of water, which would be taken from a southern well, if the money stuck to the bottom of the bowl when the water was poured off it, that that water would put away the injury if it were sprinkled on the person harmed. Well, I went myself to a well that was on the south side of my house, and I put a sixpenny piece in a bowlful of the water, but when the water was poured off the piece did not stick to the bowl; but however, I sprinkled the water on her, but though I did sprinkle it it was of no use whatever, and she never got any better. But people were saying, had the money stuck to the bowl the water would have caused the blight to be removed.")

The methods of preparation of this water undoubtedly vary, not merely because the reciters do not give the particulars, but because the operators make differences. A messenger being sent to a woman for *eolas*, we are told "she gave the one that went a bottle of water with directions that it was to be thrown on the cow."

Another reciter said that a woman being brought to see a sick cow (D. MacC.'s grandmother), "when she came she took a cog with water and went in to where the cow was. She was a decent woman, and whatever she did to the cow she got better."

In another case the local practitioner, when sent for, walked round the cow three times, and our reciter said, she may have done something more, but in any case she failed to do any good, and the cow continued ill. They then sent a messenger to another woman of the same sort, but of greater repute, and who lived at a greater distance. This woman gave the messenger a bottle of something like water, with instructions that it was to be sprinkled over the cow. When the messenger returned home and the stuff in the bottle was sprinkled on the cow, she got up, shook herself, began to show signs of recovery, and in a short time was all right.

In another case the woman sent for, "when she came said it was a case of injury by *cronachadh*, and having repeated some words over the cow, she sprinkled water she had prepared upon her with the result that the cow soon got well."

A male professor made up a bottle for a shepherd whose cow was ill, and instructed him on reaching home to sprinkle "all that was in the bottle" on certain parts of the cow. It is not advisable to take too literally statements which apparently are very exact; "all the water" in this case may simply mean the water that was in the bottle more or less in its totality. Or it may have been the instruction was so worded that if some of the water, even a drop or two, might be supposed not to have got on the cow that the charm would be ineffective. The destination of the water for particular parts of the animal was undoubtedly a usual proviso.

So far the information might lead one to suppose that an incantation said over water was sufficient in the beliefs of the operators. This is however not the case, and there can be little doubt that to make the incantation effective the water should have been in contact with silver. A native of

Harris said that he has heard of the "water of silver" as a cure for people and beasts affected by the Evil Eye, and also as a preventative of such injury if apprehended. In one instance which came under his own observation, a respectable and intelligent woman, to protect her cow and the milk and butter, first time she went to milk the cow after calving, put a half-crown piece in the bottom of the pail and drew the milk on to it. A friend who accompanied her saw the whole performance.

A native of Islay informed us that for curing eyes of those suffering from *cronachadh* you should put "three bawbees in the water"; while a native of Oban says that in all cases of *cronachadh* where water is used as a cure it must be poured on silver.

A clergyman living in Skye recently heard of a case in the parish of Kildonan where water in which silver had been immersed was sprinkled upon a cow which was unwell. The further information in this case was that the woman in the district specially referred to was exceedingly superstitious, and expressed her belief that she would become a bird after death. She always repeated a rhyme when operating upon cattle. She had died shortly before our reciter went to Skye.

A school teacher, a native of Skye and carrying on her occupation in Argyllshire, confirms the strong belief in the Evil Eye in certain places. A few years ago in D—— a young woman was driving her cow to pasture when the cow fell. Her owner turned towards a neighbour's daughter who had been looking at them passing and scolded her for the accident, finishing by stating that the onlooker was "mad." The retort was that that affliction was hereditary with the cow's owner. The interchange of compliments got the credit of curing the cow, which arose and went its way. The cure, according to this reciter, for any sudden sickness in cattle was to take a threepenny bit, or any small silver, and ask a blessing on it in the name of the Father, place it in a basin, pour water on it, and dash over the cow in the name of the Father, Son, and Holy Ghost.

In the following case the operation, though carried out by Gaelic-speaking Highlanders, was conducted in the Lowlands. A child was supposed to be the victim of *cronachadh*, and the operator was the daughter of a woman who had practised *eolas*. A fellow-servant of the operator was the reciter. "Water was procured from a running stream, it being necessary that the person bringing the water should have a piece of bread of some sort in his possession at the time. A silver coin was put in the dish in which the water was, and the operator waved the dish in a particular manner and then sprinkled some of the water on the child. The remainder was then dashed against a large stone. Stress was laid on the necessity of this part of the performance, it being essential that the stone was immovable. A solid wall, for instance the gable of a house, was said to be equally efficient. [12]

[12] If, as the writer believes, the original fluid was that mentioned in 1 Kings xiv. 10, xvi. 11, the deduction is that it should be that of a male, not a female.

Brought up in a Presbyterian community, the writer has little knowledge of the manœuvres of traditional Episcopacy or Romanism, but while speaking of this a friend, whose niece was being baptized in a hurry, gives the following information. Though the child was supposed to be dying, the officiating clergyman had first to array himself in his official costume, and then, producing a small alabaster font, prepared the water of baptism in that. Having performed the ceremony, he turned to the infant's aunt and requested to be taken to the garden, to which he himself carried the water and emptied it on the ground. Our informant, herself a Presbyterian, was speaking of the matter afterwards to the certificated nurse. She said the performance was not new to her, and told how in a like case the clergyman, not being provided with his own font, and asking for a basin, was given a nice Sèvres bowl. After the ceremony he also proceeded outside, and not only emptied out the water, but deliberately smashed the basin to prevent its subsequent use for any other purpose.

A variation in the ceremony occurred in the following case, the operator being a Lewis man. He had a nice foal which had been a good deal admired, and he was desirous of protecting it from the Evil Eye. Putting a silver coin in a dish he poured water on it. He then poured off about half of the water, apparently making a libation, and the other half he sprinkled over the foal. After this treatment he considered it would be difficult for any Evil Eye to injure it.

A native of Bernera, Harris, who can neither read nor write and has no English, shortens the process. "*Tha rathad eile anns an gabh cronachadh bhi air a chuir air falbh. Nan gabhadh neach bonn airgeid ann a' laimh agus uisge dhoirteadh air an t-airgiod agus an sin a lamh fhliuch a shuathadh air aodan an leanabh. Dheanadh sin e.*" ("There is another way in which *cronachadh* can be cured. If one takes a piece of silver in his hand and pours water on the silver and then rubs his wet hand on the child's face. That would do it.")

In tracing the accounts we have received of this Evil Eye water we started with those which seemed to deal with plain water, then with water in which one coin, and that necessarily of silver, had been placed, and now we will consider those cases where more than one coin has been used. The number seems always to be, in this case, limited to three. A native of Sutherlandshire, now resident in the mainland of Argyle, remembers as a boy accompanying an old woman to a certain well near his native place for water to be used to cure a sick child, believed to have been *air a chronachadh*. The woman had a tin can with her into which she put a sixpence, a threepenny bit, and other coins, said our informant, all silver. Before setting out he was warned that he must not speak a word, but forgetting himself he began to talk. The woman instantly stopped him, insisting that he must return home at once if he uttered another word. He kept silence after that, and when they returned with the water the woman whom he had accompanied sprinkled it on the sick child.

A native of Lochaber gives the following as the result of his own observation there. He saw different coins used, but understood that, at any rate, there should be silver. The description was given in connection with the use of the water as a diagnostic of *cronachadh*, and was as follows: The coins were put into an empty dish—a wooden one—and the water poured upon them was well water, preferably from a spring. The operator then tilted the dish over and observed whether the coin adhered to the bottom or fell away. The reciter disclaimed accurate knowledge, but said he believed if the coins adhered it was an indication of *cronachadh*, but if they fell away the illness was from some "natural" cause.

A diagnostic point with this coin water, over which however an incantation had been repeated, the words of which had not been understood by the bystanders, was made by a male practitioner of *eolas* who, sprinkling the water on some sick cows they immediately began to bellow, said that beyond doubt they had been afflicted by "witchcraft." He inquired if any milk from the cows had been supplied to others not on the farm, and when told the name of a woman so supplied, at once said that it was she who had done the mischief. Again repeating a word formula, whether the same or not, the reciter did not know, he sprinkled the rest of the water on the cows, and thereafter their milk was believed to have been quite normal.

A native of Morven giving her account of the practice there, and being a firm believer in the Evil Eye, said that the water had to be taken from a well facing the south, and the silver coin being in it, the water had to be poured into a bottle from the original dish, and the sticking of the coin to the bottom was a sign of the probable recovery of the animal for whom the water was intended.

Above it was said that three coins seemed to be the essential number when more than one was used, and we give here on the authority of a clergyman, his report of information derived from the late Mr. Stewart, the minister of Nether Lochaber. When a person is out of sorts and all overish, as they say, he is considered a proper subject for the silver water cure. A female well advanced in life is usually the operator, and she produces from her store a silver coin, the larger the coin the better, a crown piece for choice, but if it is to be had, a silver brooch with silver interlacements is even better. Getting a wooden bicker, or earthenware bowl, she goes to the nearest running water and fills her vessel from the stream to the depth that when she dips her middle finger straight down in it the water will be as high as the second joint of the finger. Having got the water she drops the coin or brooch into it, and then makes as straight a course as she can towards the place where the one is upon whom the charm is to be wrought. She must take great care that she does not spill a drop of the water by the way, and this being accomplished, the straighter the course followed the greater the omen of success. The one to be cured is now made to lie on his back—chest and neck bare—while the woman stands over him with the bowl of silver water in her left hand. Having dipped the forefinger of her right hand in the water, she makes the sign of the cross upon his forehead and in a low voice repeats an incantation. During the incantation, with her right hand she sprinkles the water on the patient seven times and as rapidly as possible. There is then only enough water left to cover the coins; this the patient is made to drink till the last drop, the bowl being tilted over till the coin touches his lips. The patient being now assured that he has been cured, is made to rise and resume his usual occupations. The words of the incantation as translated are:—

"Trinity, and might, and mercy, Holy and most merciful to human suffering and sorrow: Ever Blessed Father, loving Son of Mary, and Oh kindly Spirit of health and healing. Expel the demon of despondency and fear out of this Thy servant who believeth in Thy word.

"Holy Apostles, twelve, and Mary mother, and meek Saint Bridget, and Saint Columba too, exquisite singer of holy hymns, good and wise, intercede for him with intercession of efficacy and power. Let relief come now, and health and peace.

"Let the evil that afflicted him be driven by the winds afar: And let him arise in strength and hope and joy, to magnify the goodness of the most High.

"With water of silver, from swiftly running stream I sprinkle Thee. Arise and be well."

Unfortunately our informant was unable to give us the Gaelic words. The ceremonies here, probably having been performed in Lochaber where the Romish faith is still strong, point them back to Roman influences. There is an accuracy of description and attention to detail suggestive of the literary man very rarely to be got from popular reciters. We have however quoted our authority, one well known throughout the Highlands.

In the above there is no question of prognosticating, and the choice of the heaviest silver coin or of a silver brooch, which might be the size of a saucer, militates entirely against the chance of its sticking, even to the bottom of a wooden vessel. We are able to give a quite unembellished account of the same process from the same district by a native. "I mind one time the best cow I ever had was *air a' cronachadh*. I went for an old woman I knew who could cure beasts. She was a decent woman, and when she came she had water with her in a dish she had brought. She put a shilling in the dish, and then poured the water into another dish and turned that in which it had been upside down, but the shilling stuck to the bottom and did not fall. She struck the dish on the bottom three times with her hand, but still the shilling held on, and I had to pull it away with my fingers. The woman said that was clear enough proof that the cow had been injured by somebody's 'eye,' and she went on to heal her. She put the water on the cow's head and horns, sprinkled some all over it, and put some down its throat. In a short time the cow was all right." Compare it with the following account by a native of the parish of Urray, in Rosshire, who has seen this "silver cure" as she calls it applied both to people and beasts. She explained that it did not need a professional to do it, any one can do it for another. Here, then, we see that the virtue lies in the silver itself apparently. "Water must be taken in the name of the Trinity from where the living and the dead pass. When the water is brought home, silver, gold, and copper are put in a dish and the water poured on their top. Usually coins are used, but a gold ring or earring will do as well. The person or beast that is to be healed should be made to drink a mouthful or two of the water, and should be sprinkled all over with the rest of it. That is all that is needed for the cure. When one desires to find out if it is a case of hurt by the Evil Eye, the dish in which the water and the coins were is carefully turned over till it is mouth downwards. If the coins left in it stick to the bottom it is a sign that it was the Evil Eye that caused the trouble; if they fall away the trouble was a natural one.

Here we see a distinct reference to the Trinity, and we also notice that if we were to take that reciter's account of it all the three representatives, apparently, in order to settle the diagnosis would require to stick to the bottom of the dish.

But another reciter from the same county, but from the parish of Tarbert, makes it clear that if the silver sticks the question is settled. When the reciter's son was a baby she was living with her aunt, and one day the child began to scream as if in great pain. Nothing tried seemed to give relief, and her aunt, suspecting Evil Eye, took the reciter's marriage ring, a sixpence, and a penny, and putting them into a dish, poured water on them and then poured the water slowly off into another dish. She then turned the dish upside down. The ring and the penny came out, but the sixpence stuck, and although the bottom of the dish was struck with her hand outside, the coin still remained. This confirmed her aunt's suspicion. She said, "See you that? The child was hurt by some one envying it." The reciter added, "He was a very pretty child at any rate." The aunt gave the baby (some of?) the water to drink, and he soon got better.

A man and his wife, natives of Kinlochbervie in Sutherlandshire, separately interviewed, agree as to the common belief there in the Evil Eye and *cronachadh* generally. Mr. G. himself when a boy, being taken ill somewhat suddenly, his mother, suspecting that he had been *air a chronachadh*, got water, into which she put a gold, a silver, and a copper coin, and sprinkled the water on his face.

Mrs. H. said she has often seen it done both to cattle and people, and that it was, as well as a cure, a preventative where no suspicion of evil had already occurred, but only when it was dreaded, as, for example, in the case of young persons of prepossessing appearance.

From Back in Lewis we have evidence to the same effect, the belief in the Evil Eye being very common, and the cure by sprinkling water off the three metals usually resorted to. The reciter had seen it frequently done in the case of animals, on one occasion to a child. Application was here made to an *eolas* woman. She had water for the purpose brought from under where the living and the dead pass, put the three coins in a dish, poured the water on the metal, and sprinkled the child with the water.

The belief in the Evil Eye no doubt is pagan, though believed to be supported by Christian dogma, and seeing the importance attached to the rite of baptism in the name of the Trinity, it seems hardly to be wondered at that some equivalent ceremony should have been evolved for the cure of so mystic an influence as the Evil Eye. The writer would, he believes, be the last person to insinuate anything derogatory to one Church more than another; but using all honest material, the following statement must not be passed over.

A native of the north of Ireland, admitting the common belief in his own district in the Evil Eye, there called, as we have already stated, "blinked," informs us that the services of the priests are in demand in such cases, and it is currently reported that priests do give bottles of fluid to be sprinkled on the animals affected, with what is believed to be satisfactory result. He added that there was a story told of a man damaging his cow by using another bottle containing vitriol instead of that given by the priest. If such a thing did happen it was the man's fault, and in no way affects the question under discussion.

In reciting their incantations the practitioners also vary. The performance, as described by an eye-witness, in one case was that the woman consulted put something in a bottle, put the bottle to her mouth, spoke something into it, and then threw what was in the bottle over the cow to be cured. The result in this case was quite satisfactory, almost immediate.

In an Islay instance the woman consulted "went down to the little river that was below the houses. She had a wee dish with her, and she went on her knees and said some of the good words that she had while she was lifting the water. She took the water to where the mare was and said more of the words, and sprinkled the water over the mare." The result in this case was that the mare got better, but was never so sound as she had been before, and once she got out of the stable she never could be either forced or coaxed to enter it again, do what they would, and the attempt was frequently made.

It seems possible that the account given by one reciter of the preparation of *uisge a chronachaidh*, in which he stated that the performer takes the water to be used into his or her mouth, and from the mouth puts it into a bottle to be sprinkled from the bottle upon the person or beast to be cured, may have been a conclusion formed from the incantation process being carried on over the mouth of the bottle.

The following account, however, by a Mull woman of her own experience shows that spitting into the healing water has actually been practised. The reciter's aunt, suspecting that a cow which she had was suffering from *cronachadh*, sent her to the *eolas* woman to tell her about the beast. She found the professor in bed ill, but after giving her message the woman sent her for water to be taken from under a bridge in the neighbourhood. The living and the dead pass over this bridge, and it was always from this place that healing water for *cronachadh* was taken. While repeating the incantation she would now and again spit into the bottle, which she gave our reciter to take to her aunt. The water was sprinkled over the animal, which recovered.

Before considering water as a curative which had been in contact with other things than coin, the importance attached to silver will be made more clear by the belief put in practice that a silver coin in the pail at milking time will prevent any one taking the butter away by witchcraft. This was first noticed by a native of Ayrshire, and is practised in Islay also.

An Islay farmer and his wife being from home, the niece in charge during their absence found the churning had gone wrong. It was suggested to her to put a silver coin under the churn to counteract the action of any Evil

Eye. What the result was in that case could not be found out; but recently a cow having calved, to prevent any ill effect from the Evil Eye, a silver coin was put in her first milk, which was given to the cow herself to swallow, as soon as drawn from her.

Throughout the country at large the water prepared upon coin is undoubtedly generally known as "silver water," though we have shown that gold as well as copper—but gold more frequently—is associated with the silver. It is interesting to notice that in one account from Sutherlandshire the silver cure is described as being done with "a gold ring, and a silver coin put in a dish of water. The best dish is a wooden one with wooden hoops and no nails or iron of any kind about it." The silver coin should be "a shilling for a man, but if it is for a woman a sixpence will do."

From West Ross-shire, and from it alone, has information reached us of the use of the title "gold cure." Our informant says, "I went to see a child that was unwell, and its mother told me that she believed that it had been hurt by the Evil Eye. She said she was going to try the 'gold cure' for it, but she had no gold of any description in the house, and she asked me if I had any about me that I could lend her for the purpose. I had none at the time, so I could not oblige her, but inquired of her how it was to be used. She said she would put it in a dish of water and wash the child with the water."

STONES AND WATER

Above it was indicated that the water was put in contact with other things besides coins. In the case of the Mull woman already quoted, who had to use her butter from its unpleasant appearance for wool-greasing and such like, the *eolas* man whom she consulted put things right by getting water "and some kind of stones from a particular burn which he put in the water. It was necessary," said the reciter, "that the stones should be taken from a particular burn." She was unable to state what were the peculiar conditions which made that burn essential. The collector, who got this information in speaking to another woman in Tobermory and who believed that *cronachadh* was quite common, remembering the previous case, and hoping to draw information, suggested that certain stones were used for curing in Evil Eye cases. "Yes," said the reciter, "but there is nothing so good as three pieces of silver, three silver coins of any kind. If the water is poured on three silver coins, and the words said over either beast or body, it will cure them."

The following is a fairly circumstantial account from the parish of Clyne, Sutherlandshire, of the performance with stones and silver of a strong believer. She had a delicate daughter, and believed if people, especially strangers, looked at the girl she was sure to be ill after it, and often she would be so bad that she had to go to bed. The mother then tried the following cure, believed by many to be successful. She took a basin and put a silver coin into it, and went to a running stream near her house. From the bottom of the stream she chose seven small stones, which she put in the basin along with the coin, then dipping the basin in the stream so that the water ran into it on the top of the silver and the stones till slightly more than half full. She then went home, gave her daughter a little of the water to drink, and sprinkled a little of it on her. She kept the remainder beside her, and whenever there was any suspicion that an Evil Eye had again fallen upon her, the same process was carried out. Unfortunately the cure failed, the girl having died. It is more than probable that the weakly girl, imbued with her mother's superstition, suffered when looked at by strangers, or when she thought she was regarded with curiosity; if she had merely been nervous she would probably have been cured.

A native of Jura told how, when living with her sister there, one of the children becoming unwell an *eolas* woman was sent for, who got some stones, a darning needle, water, and other things, and with these did something to the child, but it did not recover. Our informant said they were strong in the belief that the child had been *air a cronachadh*.

Another account of the use of the darning needle comes from Ardrishaig. Our informant's grandmother had a cow grazing at the roadside, and a woman, suspected of having an Evil Eye, passing, said, "*S mart bhriagh thu, ge bi leis thu*" ("You are a bonnie cow, to whomsoever you belong"). Shortly after the cow was found "lying rolled up in a lump." "My grandmother went with a luggie for water and put a darning needle, silver, and copper into the water. She then poured some of the water down the cow's throat, rubbed her horns with the water, and sprinkled the rest all over her. In a little the cow was all right."

The same reciter mentioned another case, in which the operator was her mother. A calf became ill, and the owners were in doubts what to do with it. "My mother, remembering my grandfather's cow, put spring water in a luggie (it must be spring water) and a silver and a copper coin and a darning needle. She forced some of the water down the calf's throat, and sprinkled the rest over it. The calf recovered, and the farmer's wife was so pleased and said to my mother, 'Well, well, Mrs. S., I never saw the like of you, you can do anything.'"

No detailed description was given of the stones used, but as *clach-na-sùil*, the stone (apple) of the eye, is common Gaelic, they were doubtless of a sort more or less representative of eyes.

From Kintyre, the following information in the words of the reciter gives us some indication. "They used tae hae a bunch o' sea-shore stanes wi' holes in them hanging up at the door tae keep awa' witches." The collector had seen such stones in a house in Kintyre, but at the time did not know their purpose. They were of the honeycombed sort that may be found on shores where there are quantities of shingle. There were six or seven tied on a string hung above the inside of the inner door; they were of different sizes, guessed at from fourteen to sixteen ounces in weight.

From the island of Lewis we have another indication. There, there is a considerable amount of superstition connected with what is called *a' chlach nathrach* (the serpent's stone). The reciter, who had seen several of them, said they were usually round with one hole through them, though there may be two in some cases. The popular account of the information given was as follows: A number of serpents congregating at certain times form themselves into a knot and move round and round on the stone until a hole is worn. They then pass and repass after each other through the hole, leaving a coating of slime round the hole, which by-and-by becomes hard. It is this slime that gives to the stone the healing properties it is supposed to possess. The principal use of the stone was as a cure for the Evil Eye. Water is poured on the stone, and the person or beast affected is caused to drink the water, or has it sprinkled on them; sometimes the application is both external and internal. These stones are much prized by their possessors, who are very unwilling to part with them, and would not even willingly show them, or even acknowledge that they possessed them.

Stories of the knot of serpents being seen are still told. A very old man, a labourer, without English, and who can neither read nor write, gives the following account:—

"All the serpents in the country round about gather together to one place on one day every year, where they have a day's play. The play consists in rolling in a lump on a stone and running through a hole on the stone one after another. One time Georsa Cailean's wife (the wife of George, the son of Colin) was going home to her father, and when she was just beside a beautiful green spot near *Beinn Tartbheil* (Islay), she noticed that it was covered with serpents as thick as they could lie on the top of one another. They had gathered there that year for their play. She got a fright and ran, but if she had gone among them she would have got the serpent's stone."

A strong endeavour was made to acquire one of these stones, said to have been found in a serpent's den, but negotiations came to nothing, as the owners believing that it was good as a cure, especially for serpents' bite, refused to part with it.

It is not necessary here to discuss St. Fillan, but it is a well-known fact that the three stones, supposed to have been in his possession and kept in the meal mill at Killin, were supposed to impart healing efficacy to water in which they were steeped, and which recently, at any rate, was given to diseased cattle as a curative.

The stones principally used then are stones with an eye or eyes in them—compare usual description of the hole in the top of a needle, the eye of the needle. The stones of St. Fillan seem the nearest symbolical equivalent we have to the protruded fingers of southern Europe, which again is nearly identical with the one-eyed Fachan—the *Direach glinn Eiti* (Straight of the downy glen?) of I. F. Campbell, [13] and with which we may connect the protruded forefinger which was not to touch the yarn.

[13] "West Highland Tales," iv. 326.

IRON AND WATER

An Islay woman tells the following of her mother. "She was telling me how one time the butter went away from their milk, and for a good while they could not get a bit of butter. She was advised to go to that woman, and she went. When she told her that she could get no butter the woman took an iron and put it into the fire until it was red-hot; she then took it out and put it into a stoup of water, repeating some words at the same time. Some of this water was given to my mother to put into the churn, and would you believe it, the butter came back, and not only that, but with the very first churning there was a great quantity, equal to all that had been lost since things had gone wrong."

The reciter was a woman of about five-and-thirty, now a small farmer's wife, and well educated for her station.

The iron in this case was heated, but in another instance, in which a horse belonging to the reciter's grandfather was supposed to be injured by the Evil Eye, the *eolas* professor, a woman, having got water, dipped a bunch of keys into it and then hung the keys round the horse's neck, and sprinkled the water over the animal, repeating words which the reciter could not catch. The horse got well.

That for the cold iron, and now for the heat. "*Nan tigeadh neach a steach gus an tigh againne 'nuair a bhitheamaid a' maistreadh dhe nach biodh m'athair ro chinnteach, ghabhadh e eibhleag as an teine agus chuireadh e ann an soitheach uisg' e, agus ghleidheadh sin an toradh.*" ("If a person of whom my father would not be quite sure would come into our house when we would be churning, he would take a live ember from the fire and put it in a dish of water, and that would preserve the produce.")

As a mere suggestion, a guess for what it is worth, knowing that the old process of preparing hot water by immersing heated stones in it was practised by Highlanders, we here may have the ordinary method of scalding the churn and dishes, at one time common, become a superstitious formula.

The power of iron as protective against witchcraft, fairies, and all supernatural powers is too widespread to need special consideration. We must not however always conclude that when what is used as a means of cure is composed of iron that the iron is the principal matter. A reciter near Campbeltown gave the following information:—

"Mattie Lavarty used to be going about the country here makin' *eolas*. I mind yince a coo belongin' tae yin Neil R. took ill before calfing, an' they sent for Mattie Lavarty. She worked aboot the coo wi' water, an' said her paternoster or somethin' else o'er't an left a horseshoe in front o't. But the next mornin' whan Neil gaed intae the byre the calf was lyin' deed in the greep (byre gutter). That pit Neil frae gaun near Mattie or the like o' her ever after."

Our business here is not with Mattie's success or failure, but with the subject matter used in her attempted cure. The illness of the cow was probably a protracted labour, and Mattie put before it what was symbolical of a free passage for the expected calf. It was no mere placing of something for luck, but a use of the symbol of reproduction on an appropriate occasion.

WOOD AND WATER

The reciter in this case was a native of Tarbert, Kintyre. Believing his cow to be suffering from the Evil Eye, he sent for a practitioner of *eolas*. When she arrived, the first thing she did was to procure various kinds of wood and "different kinds of water." She made circles with a stick, repeating "words" the while. This done, she requested the owner to go out of the byre, she remaining alone in it for a considerable time. She put the water in which the wood had been steeped on the cow. The animal recovered.

It seems reasonable to conclude that the *iubhar beinne* (the juniper) would be one of the woods used, but no exact information was obtainable.

SALT AS CURE AND PREVENTATIVE

Salt is employed as a cure and preventative. The following experience of a Kintyre farmer's wife, recited by herself, gives considerable detail of the process carried out. "I mind yin o' oor ain coos was ill, an' I sent for M. McC., that was a woman beside us that had *eolas*. As shune as she seen the coo she said M. McS. was here. That was a woman folk didna' like, for they thocht she had a bad e'e. Says I: 'Ay, she was here.' 'Weel, she did harm to the coo.' She gied to the march burn and lifted water oot o't in three pairts. The first she lifted in the name o' the Father, the second in the name o' the Son, and the third in the name o' the Holy Ghost. Then she got salt and did the same wee hit. She pit the first taitie intae the bottle in the name o' the Faither, the second in the name o' the Son, and the third in the name o' the Holy Ghost. She then gied tae a corner o' the byre and prayed some prayer. When that was finished she pit the water in the coo's ears and some on her back, an' then said, 'She has plenty noo.' The coo shune got better. Peter, Paul, and Mary's names war in the prayer. She offered to learn me that *eolas*, but I didna want tae learn't."

From an Islay reciter who saw the performance we have the operation described as follows. She (the professor) first went on her knees and repeated words, then put salt on a paper. This salt she measured with a thimble painted blue in the inside. She then put it into a cloth, poured water through it into a bottle, after which she repeated words over it and gave the bottle to the man who had come to consult her about the cow.

The salt seems sometimes to be used dry. We have mentioned George — —, described as a worthy man, who was consulted to cure a cow so ill that the schoolmaster had already advised its owner to send for a man to flay it. George required that it should be put in the byre, and it had to be pulled in by main force with a rope round its horns. This being accomplished, he told the boys that they might go now and he would do the rest himself. He then asked my mother if she had salt, and when she replied that she had, he ordered her to give him the full of her hand. She gave him that, and said if there was anything he would like to have one of the children would go for it. But he answered, "This will do my business." He went back to the *bothan* (byre), and he began to work the salt in the palm of his hand. After a good while he came out and said to my mother, "Your cow is dressed now,

Flora." They then went to take her out of the *bothan*, but still she would not walk, and they had to drag her out and leave her again on the green. With this my father was after coming back, and a man along with him, to take the skin off the cow. George advised her to let her alone, for she would be all right yet. The cow recovered.

The use of urine as a preventative has been considered already. The following from an intelligent woman of about fifty, a farmer's wife in Kintyre, a well-read woman who takes an interest in things which she admittedly does not believe in, tells that when she was young, in one farm in Kintyre where she was in service, her mistress was regularly in the habit of sprinkling urine (house slops) on every cow after calving, and before she was allowed to go out, the intention being to protect the cow from the effects of the Evil Eye.

In another farm, however, in Kintyre, at the same time and for the same purpose, salt was sprinkled on every cow's back as soon as she had calved. It was an encouraging sign if the cow licked off the salt, which was specially sprinkled on either side of the rump.

It seems quite fair here to consider the salt as a more civilised representative of the other fluid, though in fact the latter is of considerable value as a cleanser under certain circumstances.

Another native of Kintyre informs us that it was a common custom at farms when the cattle were being put out on the 1st of May for the mistress to stand and throw a handful of salt on each as they passed out of the byre. She saw this done in a farm in the parish of Campbeltown, and was well aware of it being a common practice. It was avowedly done against *cronachadh*.

The writer having no skill in churning, has no knowledge what result would come from putting of salt in the churn, but an Arran woman is responsible for the statement that she had herself often seen salt put into a churn as a protection against any evil influence.

A careful observer in Islay tells how that at one time their butter having left them and they had got none for some weeks, they sent for a woman, a professor in the neighbourhood. When she came they had a churning ready to commence with, but on examining it she advised that it should be thrown to the pigs, and added that they must clean and scrub well all the dishes used for gathering the milk, and that she would return on the next day they were ready for a churning. That day having come, the *eolas* woman returned, and the first thing she did was to sprinkle a little salt on the bottom of the empty churn. The milk was then poured in and the churning commenced, with unexpectedly satisfactory results. The practitioner here was an *eolas* woman of a very good sort, and set about her operations in a manner well calculated to be successful. On the farm, however, they regarded that butter with suspicion and sold it.

To judge from what we are told in the following as having occurred in the north of Ireland, so strong is the action of salt that it will put matters right with a bad churning, even though it neither touch cream nor churn. Failing one day to get their butter properly, the reciter's master sent for an old woman in the immediate neighbourhood. When she came she just glanced at the churn, and seeing at once what was wrong, she said to the farmer, "If you like I will show you the one who has done the harm." He assured her that he did not wish that, but would be pleased if she could do anything with the churning. Without more ado, so far as W. could see, she took a handful of salt, which she threw into a pot boiling on the fire. She then gave a turn or two at the churn, and sure enough the butter came all right.

We have already mentioned the use of salt in connection with sugar as put in milk given to a woman suspected of influencing her source of supply, and from which the dairymaid took the first mouthful as a sure preventative of evil, not only for the quantity immediately given, but also for any that would be supplied subsequently during the season.

One other instance of the use of salt we give on the authority of an Arran man of about sixty-five years of age, a shrewd business man, but of whom the collector says that to judge from appearances he thinks his knowledge of the island and his family connection with it extends about as far back as the origin of the island itself.

He said his father was a great believer in the Evil Eye. One day a neighbour, walking with him while ploughing, had spoken in praise of a brown horse that was in the plough. His acquaintance had hardly left when the horse turned ill, and lay down and kicked and groaned. It was unyoked and taken home, and the Evil Eye being suspected N. R.'s wife was sent for. She came and got a mixture of salt, soot, and a lot of other things which she rubbed on the horse. She felt it all over with her hand to find out the particular spot where the eye had struck. Whatever did it, the horse recovered and was quite well afterwards.

The passing the hand over the animal to feel for material damage is peculiar. This is a usual proceeding in cases of elf-shot, but not of the Evil Eye; however, of course the woman was thoroughly entitled to make her own diagnosis in her own way.

MOST SUITABLE WATER

In the course of the preceding, various sources for water used to cure Evil Eye have been mentioned. "A certain well." This may have been a holy well of some sort, consecrated by traditional connection with some saint, though after all it may have been chosen merely to fulfil the condition mentioned elsewhere that a spring is preferable. A narrowing of the choice of springs from which water could be taken was shown in the case where one of our reciters told us that, believing the water *a bhiodh air a thoirt a tobar o'n taobh deas* (should be taken from a south well), he proceeded to take it from a well south of his own house, while another mentioned that the water required to be taken from a spring facing the south.

While roughly one-half of our reciters have expressed a preference for well or spring water, the other half prefer running water. One said "it should come from a march burn," and two mentioned "that it should be from a running stream," not mentioning any advantage to be derived from its dividing two properties. One pointed out that a piece of bread must be in the possession of the taker. In two other instances the information was given that it must be taken where the living and the dead pass. The condition further annexed that it must be from under a bridge is probably merely an expression of the reciter's own for this same idea. He would probably have considered stepping-stones, or a commonly used ford which led to a burial-place, as equally effective.

The specified qualifications really cover all the usual sources from which water can be drawn. From a native of Kintail, we hear of a case which was considered the result of the Evil Eye, though she spoke of the patient, a boy, having been "injured by some spell." He was quickly cured by the sprinkling of water from a "certain well."

An Islay reciter was very clear upon the necessity of choosing "*uisge fior*" (spring water).

From the same island, in a case where a cow was said to be suffering from "*buidseachas*" (witchcraft), which in this case seems to mean Evil Eye, the water was taken in a small tub from the Saligo River. The cow recovered, so if there is any doubt in any one's mind as to a proper source of supply, he can always procure it in the river running from Lochgorm to the west of Islay.

Another reciter said that water would be more efficacious if taken from a point where three parishes touched each other, or failing that, from a spot from which three parishes could be seen, and that he knew of water being frequently taken from a spot which answered these conditions for healing purposes of the sort we are considering. This is again an invocation of the Trinity by suggestion.

A woman who herself practised *eolas*, when asked whether it mattered what sort of water she used, said "Oh yes, it must be water from a march over which the living and dead pass." The use of this water need not apparently be accompanied by incantations and other formulæ.

A reliable informant mentioned a case which came under her own notice of a Skye woman living at Kenmore, who, having taken it into her head that a passing tramp had injured her child with the Evil Eye, "hurriedly bundling up her child, went with him to a little river near her house, and washed the boy under the bridge which was on the main road there, and the regular thoroughfare, alike for ordinary passengers and funeral processions." In fact, a running water over which the living and the dead passed.

For dwellers in towns these instructions, if carried out, might mean considerable trouble, but in one case at any rate, in Campbeltown, Kintyre, a firm believer in the Evil Eye, with a view to her own protection, "used to stand over the water tap in her own kitchen and allow the water to run while she repeated some words over the running water."

The position of some wells undoubtedly makes them fashionable. One of our informants who has lived at Crianlarich says that within the last thirty years she has known people come considerable distances to take water from a well between the old Priory and the Kirkton burying-ground, over which the "living and the dead" were wont to pass. It was taken for the purpose of curing cattle injured by an Evil Eye. A silver coin was generally in the vessel in which they carried away the water. The efficacy of this cure was commonly, if not universally, believed in by the people of the place.

TABOO WHEN IN POSSESSION OF WATER

In accordance with all the traditions of magical observance, we must expect to find the use of this curative water made dependent upon the observance of certain rules laid down by the professor. In one case already cited, a young person going with an old woman to a well for water, was ordered to keep silence, even though he himself was not carrying the water; and this was insisted upon rigidly. This was in Sutherland.

This insisting on silence is a very common taboo in other cases.

From an Arran reciter, in the case of an unmarried woman being sent for the *pisearachd*, as it is there called, the professor instructed her to go straight home, no further particulars being mentioned. This daughter of Eve and Adam sat down at the roadside and indulged her curiosity in examining what she had got from the *eolas* woman. Our reciter said, "After this, of course, it was of no use; for anything these *eolas* people give for curing should never be opened till it is going to be used. If it is opened before that, it will lose its virtue." At any rate in this case it did no good, for the cow died.

Anything approaching careful reasoning in folklore matters is not to be expected, as in religion, faith takes the first place, and reason, if admitted at all, quite a back seat. Sometimes, however, things occur which tend to diminish superstitious faith and reassert the advantage of applied reason.

In Arran, a horse was supposed to be suffering from *cronachadh*. The farmer sent a woman to get the advice of a professor, W. She had to take care of a young child at the time, and probably it was not convenient for her to leave the child at home, anyhow, she took it with her in a shawl. Having told her errand to the *eolas* man, he gave her a bottle with instructions how to use it. On her way home, constantly hitching up the child on her back, the cork came out of the bottle, and all that had been put in it was spilled. When she found this was the case she was in a "great stew" and wondered what she should do. She made up her mind that she would fill the bottle from the burn and say nothing of what had happened on reaching home if the horse did not get better; if it did she could tell the truth. She refilled her bottle, retailed the *eolas* man's instructions, the water was applied to the horse in accordance with these, and recovered. The woman now let out the secret, which, as may be supposed, somewhat shook the confidence of the public in the powers of that individual professor of *piscarachd*.

We have to take these stories as we get them. Cross-questioning the reciter has various results, from complete silence and a consequent drying-up of all information, to an acquiescence in anything they think will satisfy their interrogators. One is inclined to believe that in the following case a cracked bottle was deliberately given to the messenger so as to lead up to what happened. Our reciter said, "It was just last week I was speaking to R. G. about the man in R. One of his cows was ill, and a boy was sent to a man who cured cattle that had been *air an cronachadh*. The boy got a bottle with instructions, and was told, "I am not sure whether you will get back in time, but if the bottle does not break on the way and you can reach home before the cow dies, this will cure her." The boy went as fast as he could, but when almost home the bottle broke in halves, and all that was in it was lost. He turned back and went as quick as he could to the *eolas* man, who told him: "I knew the bottle would break, but I will make another that will not break, only I'm afraid you will not be in time." The boy hurried home to find the cow dead.

One would have supposed that any one not a fool would have looked upon this as a trick, but the reciter, a tradesman who can read and write, really an intelligent man and shrewd in other matters, added, "Was it not wonderful that he knew the bottle would break?" The collector asked him what he supposed had caused it to break. "Oh, just the strength of the evil that was inside it. One evil trying to beat another evil; the man that gave the bottle, you see, was a strong wizard." Asked to explain his idea as expressed by the one evil trying to beat the other, and was not the man who professed to cure as bad as the one who had done the harm, he explained his position by saying: "Well, no, it is right to do good and to beat the wicked one."

The spilling of the water, and consequently the impossibility of recovering it from the ground, would naturally put an end to any hope of cure from it, but it would appear that even laying it down while in the bottle deprived it of its virtue, as already pointed out.

"When myself and my father," said a reciter, "were in service at E— —, I was the herd, and one of the milch cows was attacked and not a drop of milk was left with her, but there was nothing to be seen wrong. We had a suspicion of what it was, and I went up to a worthy, clever man (*duine corr gasda*) that would be at work curing beasts that were *air an cronachadh*. When I told him what was wrong he took a bottle from the corner, while I sat by the fire. It is not known what he said on the bottle, but when giving it to me, he said: '*Air na chunnaic mi riomh gun am botal a leigeil ris a ghrunnd gus an ruiginn dhachaidh'* ('Upon what I had ever seen not to let the bottle touch the ground until I would reach home'), and upon reaching to put what was in the bottle in the cow's two ears, and he said that this would make her that she would have plenty of milk that same night. When I got home we did exactly as he had said, and the creature had plenty milk after that."

The above occurred in Islay, but the same taboo was laid on the carriage of a like medicament in Rothiemurchus. The reciter said: "My mother was for a while that she could not get any butter. Whenever she would try to gather it, it would run like sand. At last her suspicions fell on a woman in the neighbourhood believed to have the Evil Eye. My mother was advised to consult a woman supposed to have skill in these things, then resident in the parish of Rothiemurchus. When she spoke of it to my father he did not object, and said he would speak about it to the woman's husband, both being at that time at work about the laird's house. Next day the woman's husband promised my father that he would tell his wife, which he did, and she made something. I remember quite well being sent to the woman's house for the thing that was to cure the cow; my sister was with me, and the woman gave us a bottle, and what was in it was just like clear water. When giving it to us she cautioned us to be careful of it, for it must not be allowed to touch the ground until it would reach the cow; and I remember how very carefully we carried it home, and how feared we were for it. The cow was made to swallow it, and whether it was that that did it, I cannot tell, but I know they believed it was. In any case, after that the butter came all right."

The reciter of this, a woman aged about thirty-eight, was a crofter's daughter, fairly well educated and more than usually intelligent.

A very full account of the taboos to be observed by the carrier of an *eolas* cure comes from a reciter at Whiting Bay in Arran.

Two men, each having but one horse, were in the habit of doing their ploughing by uniting the pair in one team. One day both horses took ill and the Evil Eye was diagnosed. One of the owners sent for *eolas* and his horse began to recover; the other man, who at first expressed disbelief, seeing his neighbour's horse improving while his own did not, sent his niece, on the "sly," to the same practitioner, Bean A., for *pisearachd*. It is the niece who gives us the information. "Well, I went, and I told her my errand. I had a shawl on my head. When she heard my errand she went and put her hand up the lum and took something from there, and then she went into a corner and took out three wee pokes as black as soot and took something out of them. She was in the dark, but I knew that there were stones in the pokes, for I heard them rattling. She then gave me a paper with something in it, and told me that I was on no account to open the paper or let light or air into it till I would reach home. As soon as I would reach I was to tell my uncle to put what was in the paper into a bottle of water, and that he was to sprinkle the water over the horse, repeating its name three times while sprinkling it. He was then to pour a little into each of its ears, and the rest, if there should be any over, he was to put in its food. These were her directions, and I went away with the paper; but two people met me on the road and spoke to me. I did not answer them properly, for I was afraid, but just said I '*iim*,' keeping my mouth shut all the time. I had a strong wish to see what was in the paper, but was afraid if I would let in light or air it might be of no use. I resisted the temptation till I was nearly home, and then, getting behind a dyke, I put the shawl over my head in such a way that neither light nor air could get into the paper, as I thought. When I opened the paper what I saw were three wee black balls, black as soot, just like balls of soot. I never let on at home that I had opened the paper, and my uncle did all as he was ordered to do, and after a while the horse began to get better. I do not know whether it was the bottle that cured it, but it took a good while before it came to be quite well. People used to say that when a beast or body was *air a' cronachadh* it would take as long to complete the cure after the application of the *eolas* as had been between the injury and the application of the cure. Bean A. assured my uncle afterwards that it was a person of the name of Stewart that had done the harm, and there were only three of that name in the place at that time. Suspicion fixed on one of them, and by-and-by they began to cast it up to her. She got angry and went to check my aunt for reporting a thing of the kind about her. This was the first my aunt had heard of the cure, for my uncle wanted to conceal it from her, and she was very angry with him for having sent to the *eolas* woman."

In the above an express proviso was that while sprinkling the water over the horse its name was to be repeated three times. The necessity for this was expressly laid down by a Sutherlandshire reciter who said, "The person or beast to be cured is made to drink some of this (silver water), and is also sprinkled all over with some of it. The sprinkling is done in the name of the Trinity, and the name of the person or beast being operated upon must also be mentioned. This is all that is needed if it is a case of Evil Eye."

Of course there is a certain amount of pure swindle in some of these performances.

A lad was sent some miles in Islay for *eolas* for a sick cow. He gave his account of the case to the man, who then promised him a bottle. Having got the bottle and directions for its use, the messenger put it in his pocket and took his way home. Before he had got quite half-way, he fancied he heard a "commotion" in the bottle, which was still in his pocket. He then discovered that the bottle had burst (?) and what had been in it had all gone. Thinking this was not as it should be, after standing for a minute or two wondering what he should do, he made up his mind to go back and tell the scientist what had happened. Back he went, made his report, and the man said to him: "Did they manage to do that to you? I'll give you a bottle they cannot break." He got another bottle ready, waved his hands over it before giving it to the lad, saying as he did so, "Here, *they* cannot break this one, but the cow will not be saved." He told the boy who had injured the cow. *They* were the doers of the evil, evidently supposed to be acting with intention to do injury; so this case might be considered as one of witchcraft by those concerned in it.

WATER, WHERE APPLIED

There has been already occasion to mention that the instruction given with the healing water was to make the animal swallow some of it, but yet more frequently to sprinkle it on the beast. The most usual locality, however, to which it is ordered to be applied is that of the ears.

A reciter's father-in-law had a sick horse which was supposed to have eaten or drunk nothing for some days. A woman in the neighbourhood was consulted, who, when she came into the stable, put some water (?) in the ear of the horse, saying some words at the same time. The horse, which was lying down, rose to its feet, began to eat, and recovered.

Another reciter told of her own husband, who got something in a bottle, which he was ordered to put a portion of in the horse's ears, and to sprinkle some all over its body. As soon as he came home he did what he had been ordered, the sick horse rose to its feet, began to eat, and completely recovered.

In another case the reciter's father had a grey horse which he described as not being *uamhasach bochd* (frightfully bad), but it would not eat. To tempt the horse it was allowed in among their standing oats, but it would not bend its head to eat a bite. His father, taking the advice of another, went to J. R.'s grandmother and told her how the matter was. She assured him she would not be long in giving him what was wanted; she then gave him a bottle with the instruction, "*A chuir a cheud da spuit dhe na bha 'sa bhotal, aon anns gach cluais dhe 'n t-ainmhidh, agus an corr a chrathadh sios air a mhuidh, agus air a dhruim agus leigeil leis sruthadh sios air.*" (To put the first two spouts of what was in the bottle one in each ear of the horse, and to sprinkle the remainder down on his mane and on his back, and allow it to run down on him.) In this case also the horse gave himself a shake, began to eat, and recovered.

The same formula was applied to cattle. A Kintyre farmer had a sick cow, and was advised to consult an *eolas* woman in the neighbourhood. Having no faith in that sort of thing, it was some time before he consented, but he did at last on the plea that it could do no harm. The woman being sent for, procured water and salt; these she put into the cow's ear, reciting some unintelligible form of words. The cow seemed to brisk up at once, and the result was so satisfactory that the owner's sister-in-law, who was present at the performance and had previously taken up a position of unbelief, said to him, "I think, J., there is something in it after all."

We have already given the particulars of how two beautiful quey calves were affected by the Evil Eye of a woman who stared at them over the field dyke. One died, but the other was cured by what appeared to be pure water which the owner was told to put in the ear of the sick calf. When this was done it shook its head, got on its feet, and recovered.

These cases all get the credit of being recoveries. But a Dumbartonshire case was less successful. When the reciter was in service one of the cows took ill, and old J. W., who was always in the byres and well acquainted with cattle, insisted that the beast was ill from the influence of some one *aig am bheil droch shuil* (who had an Evil Eye). Nothing would satisfy him till a woman, A. T., was sent for. She did not find it convenient to come herself, but sent a bottle with water in it, instructing the messenger how to put it in the cow's ear. The instructions were carefully carried out, but the cow died.

Any person who had been made to shudder by the inside of the ear being tickled, would see at once how the animal was recalled to activity.

The following, from a native of Tiree, shows either that he had forgotten the instruction given to put the water directly into the ears, or the professor, while still remembering the shaking of the head as sign of returning activity, had contented himself with the simple sprinkling. It was the reciter's cousin who went to the *eolas* man, and who, having "made up a bottle," told him to sprinkle it on the horse when he would reach home; and if it would shake its ears when the stuff would go on it, he said it would live, but if not they need do no more, for it would die. Our information was that the thing was done according to the directions given, as soon as the horse felt the water it shook its ears, and as the *eolas* man had said, recovered.

ODD CURES

There are some odd cures mentioned in individual cases.

HONEYSUCKLE CURE

From a good correspondent in the North of Argyllshire comes the following account of a clerk in a factor's office. He complained at times, and certainly did not look very well, but not much attention was paid to him, as any illness he had did not seem serious. "A frail old woman came into his parents' house one evening as the lad returned to supper. She looked at him keenly, waited till he went out, and then asked, 'What is he complaining of?' His mother was surprised, but answered that he was feeling the confinement in his office a good deal, but that there was not much wrong. 'You need not tell me that,' said the old woman, 'I can easily see there is something very real the matter with him. Some one has laid their Evil Eye upon him. I'll tell you what you should do. Go to the woods, get a good long bit of the *iadh-shlait*, take it and twist it this way round his whole body, repeating the following words, and you will see your son hale and hearty soon.' The lad's mother did not believe in the cure and did not try it, nor could she give the words recommended to be used." The plant here is the honeysuckle, the Gaelic name given being used for it alone in the district. Dictionaries, however, say that it is also used for "ivy," which in those parts as elsewhere is called *eitheann*.

CAT CURE

The reciter, a probationer of the Free Church and well up in folklore matters, when in Harris, of which he was a native, heard of the following. A man's cow was taken suddenly ill, and the only conclusion they could come to was that it was a case of Evil Eye. The owner of the cow, acting on advice, took a cat and rubbed it on the cow. The cow recovered.

RUBBING HAIR THE WRONG WAY

The reciter's grandfather was a Stratherrick man (Loch Ness), and when attending the market there, was approached by another man to sell him a stirk. There was a good deal of bargaining. No agreement was come to, the offerer leaving as if dissatisfied. Before the market closed the stirk fell to the ground and could not be got to rise. F.'s suspicions of course fell upon the rejected offerer. An acquaintance who also was attending the market, and was supposed to have eolas, happened to come about, and seeing F. in distress reassured him: "*Cha'n eagal do'n bheachan a laochain.*" ("No fears of the beast, my lad.") He then drew the palm of his hand up the stirk's back against the hair, repeating words which the reciter, however, had never heard. The stirk got on its feet and was soon brisk and well.

CHANGING THE FIREPLACE

"There was a man living in Machri whose cattle and horses were dying, and things generally going against him. He knew quite well it was the Evil Eye, so he consulted a *buidseach*. The *buidseach* told him to change his fire to the other end of the house. Having done this his cattle recovered, and he was prosperous ever after."

Unfortunately this is the whole information available. The cattle not improbably were housed beneath the same roof as himself; but it would be of no benefit speculating as to the effect of changing the fireplace nearer to or farther from his stock. All that can be said is that the change of position of the fireplace was credited with a change in the man's luck.

THE POWER OF A CHILD'S MUTCH

Whether the child in this case was suffering directly from the Evil Eye the reciter was not prepared to say.

In the neighbourhood of Tayinloan, Kintyre, there were several women who professed to be able to cure sicknesses arising from the Evil Eye. One of these women was sent for in the case of a child thought to be dying. When she arrived the household were gathered round the child, thinking he was approaching immediate death. When the woman looked at him she said nothing, but asked for a child's mutch (close cap), and when it was given her she went outside, repeated a charm over it, and returning, put the mutch on the child's head and said he would soon be well. In a little while he kicked and stretched himself, and it was not long till he was all right.

WHISKY CURE

In only one case have we heard of this universal solvent of misfortune being used as a cure for the Evil Eye. The churning was unsuccessful; the dairymaid was convinced that it was a case of Evil Eye, and advised that a glass of whisky should be put in the churn. The advice was not taken, so we have still to learn the effects of whisky in like case. This was in Caithness-shire, where belief in the Evil Eye is very common.

LEAD DROPPING

We have already considered the reference of the diagnosis to the augury of a piece of silver sticking to the bottom of a dish. All sorts of prognostications are got by pouring albumen of eggs into water as well as melted lead; the latter was used in the following instance of what it disclosed as a case of Evil Eye.

The reciter was a well-educated sick-nurse, of middle age and thoroughly reliable. A girl had taken suddenly ill. A young man in the neighbourhood was desirous of marrying her, but the suitor was not acceptable, and the girl took every opportunity of letting this be seen. A neighbour, supposed to have special skill and whose method of hanky-panky was the dropping of melted lead into water, was consulted. She went through her performance and showed the lead, part of it at least, in the form of a heart with a hole through it. She explained to the sick girl, "Look at that, his eye is in you and you are far better to take him." The match was made, and the girl recovered her health. The same woman, going through the same performance with reference to a sick lad, showed to his aunt and sister some of the lead in the form of a coffin, and from that pronounced the case hopeless. The lad shortly thereafter died.

In the case of the pierced heart, there is no doubt, the idea on the part of the reciter was that actual illness was brought on by the desirous eye of the young man, not merely that the lad had an eye to her as a satisfactory partner.

AN EYE FOR AN EYE

We have pointed out that the belief in an Evil Eye is founded upon a literal acceptance apparently of the validity of the commandment "Thou shalt not covet." To the writer this seems the hardest of the Decalogue. It forbids thoughts which pass involuntarily through the mind. A person to whom Nature has given an ambitious and acquisitive disposition breaks this commandment necessarily, however openhanded may be his practice. With all reverence, the commandment seems to be a pushing into the region of thought what has been forbidden in practice by the commandment "Thou shalt not steal." No doubt to covet means more than a simple liking to possess, and it is the inordinate, the excessive desire which is forbidden. The theory of the Evil Eye as demonstrated in the beliefs of the West Highlanders shown here may have sprung entirely, and owe their origin to, if not the tenth commandment of the Decalogue, an acceptance as valid of the instruction therein contained. The acceptance of this commandment as binding, demonstrates that there is a power for evil in thought alone. The covetous man's eye is "in it," let him do as he likes. This power is shown vividly by the belief so often expressed that admiration of one's own possessions will result in evil to them.

To counteract this deleterious result the possible sufferer has to be put under the protection of a higher Power, and so, if the person coveting remembers, a simple "God bless" will ward off evil. But the Evil Eye is not the sole property of the active-minded Christian, and even when it is so it is not necessarily a simple matter to suggest to him that he is breaking the tenth commandment; in fact there may be a difference of opinion on the matter, and it will not do to leave to the other's goodwill your security from loss and damage. A curative ritual has been excogitated. In these ceremonies the Trinity is frequently made, or, let us say, called on to take a part. The curative water is prepared on three metals—gold, silver, and copper—the magic thread has three knots on it, and sickness thus divided into three is destroyed, say by burning two portions, one in the name of the Father, the other of the Son, while that given over to the influence of the Holy Spirit, which may be naturally supposed to counteract the covetous instinct, remains attached to the sufferer in the third and unburned knot. To show that this symbolism is carried out fairly consistently, we would call attention here to the use of the three-knot charm in the procuring for sailors of a favouring breeze. Readers must take it on our authority that there are numberless accounts of the giving of a three-knotted thread for this purpose, and the usual instructions for its use fully bear out our contention. After starting one knot is to be unloosed, and the breeze will be favouring and probably gentle. To expedite matters the second knot may be untied, and the result will be increase in the force of the favouring wind, but on no account must the third knot be interfered with, or the breeze will rise to a gale, and none will be able to answer for the effect. Compare the above statement with what appears in the Gospel of St. John iii. 8: "The wind bloweth where it listeth, and thou hearest the sound thereof, but canst not tell whence it cometh, and whither it goeth: so is every one that is born of the Spirit." Add to this Genesis i. 2: "And the Spirit of God moved upon the face of the waters."

This is not to be considered as a reasonable deduction from the texts quoted. It merely shows that the authority may seem to give support to a connection being suggested as existing between the Spirit of God, and the Holy Spirit of the Trinity, and the uncertainty and force of the wind which is put under its governance.

But when we come to symbols and metaphors we open a wide field which need not be restricted by what is within the domain of the Church. The fact stares us in the face that the *uisge a chronachaidh* (the water of (against) injury) is more frequently prepared from one metal—silver—even than from three. It is in fact frequently called Silver Water. There can be here no traceable connection with a Trinity. The idea seems to be that the white metal represents an eye. Seeing that the principal medium of exchange among the people is silver, as things go, it is not very far fetched to make a silver coin stand for what is acknowledged to be hurtful from the point of view of covetousness, seeing that St. Paul tells us, 1 Timothy vi. 10, that "the love of money is the root of all evil." Having this in mind, we can easily see how the adherence of a silver coin to the bottom of a wooden or other vessel comes to be relied on as settling the cause of an illness, whether it be the Evil Eye or something else. The round white coin staring at you, as it were, from the bottom of the cogue says "Eye" as distinctly as it is possible. If it does not adhere no suggestion of an eye is made, consequently the sickness in question arises from something else. We do not hear of a copper, and very rarely of a gold coin being used by itself. We hear of gold being used in the form of the marriage ring, but the symbolism here is the same as in the serpent stones and the honeycombed stones in Kintyre, it represents an eye by its form.

A reciter from the Chanonry, Ross-shire, says he has frequently seen women take the ring off their finger, and hurriedly putting water on it in a dish, dash the water over their children if they saw a person coming to call about whom they had any suspicion. This was with a view to prevent *cronachadh*, either witchcraft or the Evil Eye.

This connection with an eye explains also how the giving away of a darning needle means the giving away of one's luck. This seems somewhat peculiar to the island of Arran. We give the following as a sample:—

An Arran reciter said: "Bettie many a time tells me of a woman they have beside them who never darns stockings or anything else. One day this woman came in and asked Bettie for a darning needle. Bettie suspected it was for no good end she wanted it and would have refused it, but the woman having seen it went and took it with her. For some time thereafter Bettie was very unlucky. Things were going against her, and one night she dreamed that somebody came to her and said, 'Why did you give away your darning needle? You have given away your luck with it.' When she got up in the morning she just went into the woman's house, and seeing the darning needle stuck in a pincushion, she went and took it with her."

Bettie here had given away the magic eye of its owner, which acted as a counter charm to the Evil Eyes of others. The above is not the only power inherent in a darning needle in Arran. There, stuck in the cap or bonnet, it is as complete protection against the under-world as represented by fairies, as elsewhere a knife is frequently quoted as being.

SHOWING WHO IS THE MISCHIEF MAKER

We are so easily content to waive aside these superstitions when they come in our way, as if they were the unconsidered dreamings of the insane. Not one of them but has its origin, generally no doubt in a misguided fancy, but still based on something real enough to the mind of the believer, even if it be a mind of childlike simplicity. But when *eolas* men and women take on themselves to find out for the instruction of their clients to whom the Evil Eye damaging them belongs, one begins to doubt but that there is more of the wisdom of the serpent than of the simplicity of the dove in this part of their performance. We have already mentioned a case in which the *eolas* woman described to the reciter's cousin "exactly" the man and woman who had harmed her child, though neither man nor woman had been mentioned to her, and the reciter expressed wonder at the knowledge so displayed.

This spotting the doer is evidently a little more difficult of belief to many than the other notions they entertain about the Evil Eye. Thus, a reciter says that one professor confirmed the owner's suspicions, a fact openly admitted, but added, "It was said that she told them whose eye had taken the milk away." In another, "It was believed he could also tell who had done the mischief?"

But in some cases the individual is straightforwardly given. Five reciters at least mentioned that, and in one of these the reciter accepted the nomination as indubitable because they had met "the very man she mentioned on the road."

There can be no doubt that some of these *eolas* people have deliberately offered to disclose the personality of the one doing the harm. The owners of the sick animal have refused to have such information given them, stating that they would be entirely content with a cure without knowing any ill of a neighbour. Refinement of feeling of this sort is foreign to many, however, and indeed it is to be excused in a thorough believer, if for no other reason than the well-known principle that "prevention is better than cure." Some of the indications are particularly vague.

"He asked if a dark-haired man had been praising the cow, and when they said that they didn't know, 'Well,' said he, 'it was a man with black hair (*ceann dubh*) that injured your cow, with the Evil Eye!'"

In another case the identified doer, as previously mentioned, had brown hair.

In some cases, though no names are mentioned, it is quite clear that identification was intended. Thus, in one of the cases cured by a cord, the professor stated that the child had been injured by a mother and her daughter. "My man said that that was quite true, but that they had no ill-will to us, and why should they do that?" To that the woman said, "That it was likely that they did not know themselves that they were doing it."

In another thread-cured case, the man operating said that it had been injured by drovers who wanted to buy the animal in question. We may conclude that the *eolas* man knew that drovers had been in the neighbourhood.

Similar cases have already been mentioned, the particularity of the description pretty clearly demonstrating that the professor would have been more candid if, instead of asking whether a dark and a fair woman with a blue shawl had been calling, they had said there had been, and that they were responsible.

But this describing the individual without naming him is evidently a trick of the trade. A farmer's wife consulting an *eolas* man without at first the consent of the farmer, the professor described to the couple the appearance of the man who had done the mischief. We then learn that from the description they knew at once who the man was, and also that he had been in the byre shortly before the cow had taken ill.

It was probably a safe enough decision to credit strange drovers with an injury of the sort, their stay in the district being of course but a temporary one; but one suspects local jealousy in the following case, when a woman, desirous of getting back her vanished butter, was told that those doing the injury were not a musket-shot from her house. This was in Islay, and some Jura people staying in the neighbourhood, it was concluded they were those pointed at.

A parallel appears in the case already mentioned, where all Tiree *cailleachs* are slumped as dangerous. One suspects that in the following case an undesirable neighbour had been suggested.

There were three farmers side by side in the parish of Kilbrandon. The one in the centre was not nearly so successful as his neighbours. The unfortunate farmer went to A— — to consult a certain *eolas* man. By him he was told it was no wonder he was not getting on, for he had on each side of him "those who were doing him harm, and until he would remove he would never get on." Taking the hint he looked about him, removed to another farm, and succeeded very well.

When in doubt, the professor, in some cases at any rate, acquires by examination assurance of the presence of an individual to accuse. Having put the string on a sick cow and the cow being cured apparently, "she (the *eolas* woman) came to the lassie that had been herding the cow and said to her: 'You saw a man among the cows to-day, and you heard him saying that that cow was a good one.'" The girl said, "Yes." The woman then said: "The man was J. G.," and the girl again said, "Yes." The woman then told them that it was the said J. G. who had done the harm. They all knew him quite well. "And now," added Mrs. M. in telling her story, "if that woman had no knowledge, how could she have known who had been among the cows on that day, or who had done the mischief."

In some cases a description is given of a method of identification of the owner of the Evil Eye. Formerly we described how a woman consulted shut her eyes, and opening them after an interval, informed her interrogator that anything she saw of the nature of a burden was what was pressing on the sick animal. In that instance it was said to be a horse collar.

Probably in this case the woman satisfied herself of the gravity of the illness by comparing it with the relative weight of the burden.

In another case in which Thursday and Sunday were said to be the lucky days for the preparation of the *uisge a chronachaidh*, and it took from Wednesday to Sunday to prepare the stuff, the blame was at the end of that time laid to the charge of a stranger from Tiree. One can scarcely doubt that in that case the time was utilised to make inquiries.

In addition to these more crude methods there are indications of the dark-room business carried on in more civilised places almost to the present day. There was a man who lived at Balloch in the island of Lewis much consulted, and believed to be specially skilful in dealing with cases of the Evil Eye. "For a consideration he would produce the likeness of those who had done the harm, showing it to the injured. He would take them into a little room he had, where he would show them the likeness of the owner of the Evil Eye."

Another traditional method of identification was "to make some one pass before the inquirer, and the one who had done the harm would be of the same name." We say traditional in this case, because we have no information about smoke-raising, crystal balls, or anything of the kind, and are therefore inclined to refer it back to the Biblical account of Saul's interview with Samuel.

That the story of the magic mirror has found its way into the Western Highlands, however, is made clear by the following. A lighthouse-keeper is our informant.

Five men meeting his neighbour outside the lighthouse stopped him and informed him that having left their boat on the beach, when they went back to it they found it had a hole, and they wished to see in the looking-glass who had done the mischief. When the lighthouse-keeper assured them that he had no such looking-glass, and expressed astonishment that they would believe in such nonsense, they seemed somewhat displeased. In recounting this incident afterwards the light-keepers learned that an impression had gone abroad in the place that there was a particular mirror at the station that had the property of showing who those were that had taken part in cases of witchcraft. It is easily comprehensible how the reflectors in a lighthouse might be spoken of as of peculiar efficacy, with the usual "Three Crows" result.

The difficulty of course is to distinguish between claims advanced of the possession of a power, of which, under the circumstances, a demonstration cannot be demanded, and the actual carrying out of some impressive hanky-panky. The following is an illustration:—

A messenger being sent for a cure, and having received it, the scientist told him that if the cow had been his own she could make the shadow (*faileas*) of the one who had done the mischief to pass before him, or, if the woman who was the owner of the cow had come, she could have done it for her.

One can scarcely be accused of a want of Christian charity if he suggests that if the professor had had the owner before him he would not have claimed the powers he did.

In the story already related of Campbell of Skipness showing the injurious one in a carefully darkened barn, the reciter, also a Campbell, had all the appearance of believing in the story, but as it was told of a relative of his great-grandfather's, no one can say what are the accretions time has added to the facts of the case.

We have pointed out that even the Church has been brought in contact with the Evil Eye scientist, and the following information from a well-informed, clever, middle-aged lady, the sister of a clergyman whose father took an interest in traditional Gaelic matters, as she does herself, was heard from a Sutherlandshire minister who recited it to her mother. The milk of their cows being unsatisfactory, the housekeeper asked leave to consult an *eolas* man. The minister was very angry, but the housekeeper stuck to her text and carried out her purpose, telling the minister, "*Na gabhadh sibhse gnothuch sam bith leis, agus chi mise de ni mi.*" ("Take you nothing to do with it, and I'll see what I'll do.") She got the *eolas* man, and he asked for a basin of the sort of watery stuff they were getting instead of milk. When he got it he closed up every hole and crevice, even stuffing up the key-hole. Then he put the milky water on the fire, and when it was hot he took a knife and began to cut with it through the pot of milk. While at this work a woman came to the door, screamed, and wanted to get in; but he cried to her that he would give her plenty of it, and he continued cutting away through the milk. Still she screamed and begged him to let her come in, but he said he would not until she would promise to give up her wicked work and give the *toradh* back to the minister's cow, all the time continuing cutting with the knife. She answered she would promise everything he wanted, for every cut of the knife was going through her heart. The man then opened the door and took the pot off the fire, and from that time the supply of milk, both for quantity and quality, was satisfactory. In this case also, though the authority is thoroughly respectable, it is impossible to say what actually took place. In fact it may be that our informant may have mistaken a traditional recitation as the experience of the reciter himself. Though told àpropos of the Evil Eye, looking at the story in all its bearings, it looks as if it had been, if it happened at all, a case of pull devil pull baker between two witches, one of whom was supposed to be taking the minister's milk.

But your witch, male or female, still exists, and his presence probably does not conduce to harmony in his neighbourhood. Two brothers lived beside the father of our reciter in J——. They had a bit of land between them, and their dwelling-houses stood end to end under one roof. The wife of the one brother suspected the wife of the other of injuriously affecting her dairy products by the Evil Eye. She persuaded her husband to take her part, and he crossed to I—— to consult one having the reputation of witchcraft there. The witch resolved to go in person to examine into the matter, and he accompanied the man home, where he assured the couple who considered themselves injured that he would bring the injurer crying to their door. The suspected woman, already much annoyed, sent for the reciter's mother to come to her, who found her sitting in tears. The visitor encouraged her, told her it was all nonsense and advised her not to be downcast, and returned home. Shortly thereafter she had a visit from the woman complaining, who told her with glee that the man consulted had put them on a plan for finding out who was injuring their milk. The mutual friend received this information coldly, and proceeded to point out that there were no grounds for suspecting any one outside her own house, and advised her to go home, well clean her dishes and keep her eye on her daughter, assuring her that if she did that she would probably have satisfaction with her milk and cream. The result was quite satisfactory, as it turned out to be as suspected, that the daughter helped herself in her mother's absence.

PUTTING ELSEWHERE

The procedure of the *eolas* woman in Bernera (Harris), given above, burning two of the knots of the charmed string to carry off the disease, stating as she put each knot in the fire, "The disease and the sickness I would put on the top of the fire," it is evident that the evil was treated as something capable of being destroyed, in that case by the action of fire. The same idea appears in the following: —

The reciter remembered when misfortune came to their cattle. One cow after another died, and then a horse died, and her brother, a good deal older than herself, saying he could stand it no longer, went to consult an *eolas* man. The latter professed to understand the case, said it was an Evil Eye that had done the mischief, and offered there and then to make the individual appear before him so that he would know who it was. Her brother refused to accept this offer, and the proposition made to him then was that the illness should be transferred to the cattle of the wrong-doer. This also met with disapproval, and then it was proposed that the illness should be thrown in the sea. The cure in this case was connected with waving the tether over the sick horse.

In another Islay case where the *dosgach* was supposed to have come to the locality with a newlymarried wife of one of two brothers, a reputed curer was consulted. He made out that it was a case of *buidseachas,* and he offered to put the *dosgach* on any of the consulters' neighbours' cattle. This did not meet with the farmer's approval, as he was unwilling that his neighbours should suffer, so he declined to mention any name, but recommended that the evil effect should be put in the sea. One can scarcely doubt that, there being cattle sickness in the district, the chances were in favour of the cattle of any named person being affected, so that even if the offer had been accepted and the farmer committed himself as desiring harm to his neighbour, the *eolas* man's credit or discredit would have been maintained. He must by this time have had a fair idea of the disposition of the man he was dealing with, and probably expected that his offer next made to show him for half-a-crown the individual in fault would be refused. It was so, and the reciter gave the reason for this refusal, viz. that it would be *an t-aibhisdear* (the adversary, the devil), who would appear in the likeness of a man. This explains sufficiently the reason influencing those who refuse such offers, even if one did see an appearance which was recognisable. The evidence that the individual shown did it was unreliable. The devil has been a deceiver from the beginning, and if the vision was that of him masquerading, doubtless for his own purposes, he might be deceiving the inquirer.

The above story was told by the daughter of one of the two brothers concerned, and she vouches for the truth of it, having heard her father and uncle talk of it often and often. She added a curious incident, which seems to have had something to do with the diagnosis of the case. The man consulted the "Red Witch," as he was called, and sent the farmer back "for the twelve points of the sick cow." It was explained that this meant the tips of the horns, ears, hoofs, &c. These were examined, and the opinion expressed that the cow could not be cured, for the mischief had got too near her heart, but it could be lifted from all the rest, so that it would not trouble them any more. She further explained that they were led to understand that it was two brothers who were doing the harm, and we notice that it was two brothers who were consulting the witch doctor. She said that the sickness was put into the sea.

From another case we get information of how this could be done. "A stirk of my father's was ill, and we sent to a man for a cure. He sent a bottle with instructions that part of it was to be sprinkled on the stirk, and the rest thrown into the sea. As soon as what was in the bottle went on the beast, its horns got warm. We threw the rest of the stuff into the sea as ordered, and after that the stirk got quite well."

It has been pointed out already that there is no witchcraft necessary to the Evil Eye, but that the processes for its cure undoubtedly are witchcraft. The following will show the idea prevalent as to the powers of transferring illness.

The reciter, an Islay woman, said: "There was a lad at service with Malcolm here beside us. He was one of the T.'s. He used to come our way, and my father said to me not to have too much to do with him, for there was something wrong about him (hereditary witch power). Well, while that lad was beside us every foal that we had died. One day my father went towards the march between ourselves and Malcolm. It was pretty early, and he noticed the dog sniffing between two little hillocks there. He went over to see what the dog was at, and what did he find but a foal's head buried under the ground. It was the head of a foal of Malcolm's that had died, and the lad had buried it at our march to put the trouble upon us. My father was terribly angry (*fuasach angrach*), for he would not do the like to another man. He lifted the head and threw it into a drain, where it would not do any harm and away from every man. *Ach coma leibh* (but all the same), the time of one of our mares was out, and when she cast (her foal), what was there but two heads on the foal." The reciter went on to say that that lad left Malcolm and went to Fair Peter, but Peter got his burning with him, for while he was with him the foals were dying on him, Besides the harm that was done to what belonged to his master, he (the lad) got a piece of a dead calf and put it on a neighbour's land, and with this that neighbour's calves "began to go on him."

This story was told apparently with full belief, and the only conclusion we can draw from it, seems either that some cattle sickness prevailing in the neighbourhood was credited to the unfortunate lad, or else that for some revengeful or other purpose of his own he had damaged the stock of his master.

We have another account of the same belief from a native of Kilbrandon, Seil Island, where a belief in the Evil Eye was exceedingly common. He said: "When a beast dies, there being a suspicion that the death has been caused by such an Eye, the owner buries it stealthily, not on his own ground, but on the ground of some other person, the idea being that if buried on his own ground the influence of the Evil Eye would be likely to remain, and he might lose still more beasts, but by burying the animal on the ground of another he transfers the evil from himself to the person on whose land it was buried." The reciter knew of the following instance of this:—

A very superstitious family, who believed in and were much afraid of witchcraft and the Evil Eye, lost some of their beasts and were quite sure that the Evil Eye was the cause of death. The head of the family, watching a convenient opportunity, went at night and buried them in the dunghill of another man who lived a distance of about two miles from him. No one knew this at the time, and it was only when putting out the manure they found the remains of the beasts and came to know that they had been buried there.

It would be unfair to encourage the belief that the professors of *eolas* always give themselves to spreading evil reports of neighbours. One being called in where the butter supply was unsatisfactory, after advising the use of earthenware dishes in preference to wooden ones for gathering the milk, the dairymaid asked if she could tell her who had taken the *toradh*. The answer was, "Is not your name A.?" On being answered that that was so, the *eolas* woman said, "It may have been yourself."

APPENDIX

An attempt has been made to give an honest account without literary varnish of the present-day influence of the belief in an Evil Eye in the Gaelic-speaking districts of Scotland. It is difficult to be certain that nothing of moment has escaped observation. The influence of Bible texts, no doubt used divorced from their contexts generally, as well as the protective power of the Divinity, have been pointed out as influencing the superstitious. One other instance we would give from the island of Luing, which has been handed in since the rest has been in type.

The reciter said: "I knew a real good woman who always, when the first meal of the season was got from the mill, sent a pitcherful of it here and there to the poor people round about. But there were some to whom she would give none, because she suspected them of having evil in their hearts, and that if they got a pitcherful they could take all the strength out of what she kept for her house use. You see, Hezekiah should not have shown the King of Babylon all his treasures." Compare 2 Kings xx. 12-19, and Isaiah xxxix. Evidently the idea was that the King of Babylon was envious of Hezekiah's possessions, as the others might have been of the good lady's meal.

Mention has been made of the belief that the Evil Eye could split the rocks themselves. A traditional account of such an incident comes from the island of Coll. "One time a man was carrying a quern (hand corn-mill) on his back in a poke, and was met by a servant of St. Columba. Thinking the quern was a cheese, he coveted it, and when the man came to take it out of the bag he found it in two. Columba said of it, '*B'e farmad na suil a bhris a' chlach*.'('It was the envy of the eye that broke the stone.')" The same story reached us at the same time from a Breadalbane source. A local laird who hurt his own cattle, and whose dairymaid had to slam the byre door in his face, met a girl on her way home from the shieling. The girl had a quern (*muileann brath*) in a bag on her back. When she passed the laird looked after her, and supposing what she was carrying was a *ceapag caise* (a small cheese), he put his eye in it. When the girl reached home the mill-stone was in halves, his Evil Eye had broken it.

Some verses describing the powers of a certain Macandeoir, give us a lesson in popular comparative philology:—

"*A Mhurach biorach lom na suil olc.*

Gonadh thu maigheach's a fhiadh.

Gonadh thu 't-iasg a bhiodh 'san loch

Nuair a shealladh thu orra gu dlu.

Latha caogda thu d shuil a bha olc,

Cha bhiodh luathas 'nan cleith

'S bhiodh gach creutair dhiudh na'n corp.

A Mhurach Macandeoir

Gonadh thu Para Caimbeal

Gonadh thu' shleisdean 'sa chnamhan.

'S d' fhag thu e bioradh fann."

("Oh Murdoch, piercing, bare, of the bad eye,

You would wound hare and the deer.

You would wound the fish that would be in the loch

When you looked closely at them.

The day you cocked (winked) your wicked eye

There would be no motion (quick movement) in their bosom

And each creature of them a corpse.

Murdoch Macandeoir

You would pierce Para Campbell,

You would pierce his thighs and his bones

And you left him wounded, weak.")

The respected correspondent who sends this and the writer differed as to the word here translated "wound." The original spelling suggested that *gonadh* was the word, and it corresponds with the other information received in like cases, but the reciter explained, and sticks to it, that it means "to covet." Now the word *gionach* means "greedy" "gluttonous," and *gonadh* means "wounding" "bewitching," thus, *gonadh ort* is a form of imprecation. The philologist will tell us they have nothing to do with each other, and this may be admitted from his point of view, but not from the popular one.

Murdoch here immortalised was credited with the power of destroying the winter supply of beef, even after the slaughter of the animal. "When I was a little lad, my father and my uncle William bought a cow from him in winter. It was customary to buy a fat cow, kill it, and divide it so as to have a cheap and good supply. The beast was killed and hung in the barn. The same day Murdoch passed, and they knew that on returning he would call to see how the animal bought from himself turned out after killing. They were in a fix to prevent his seeing her without offending him, and the plan they took was to close the barn, locking the door and giving the key to some one who, if inquiries were made, would not tell where it was. Murdoch called, asked if the cow was killed, and said he wanted to see her. They then proceeded to the barn, but of course could not get in. An apparent search was then made for the missing key, which naturally they could not find. Murdoch was disappointed, but asked if she had killed well. They said she had, and expressed regret that they could not let him see her. So they prevented him laying his eye upon her after killing; before that, while she was his own, of course his eye would not harm her." The latter remark is not in accordance with the belief in other places.

A native of Bute enables us to give another illustration of care taken to keep an Evil Eye from dead meat. A woman of whom, as our reciter said, there could be no doubt she had a "bad eye," asked some fishers to take her along the coast in their boat. Not liking to refuse, they agreed. They had a fine catch of salmon with them at the time, which she praised loudly as they lay in the net at her feet. "Well, for many a day after that we got no good from that net. We might every bit as well look to the hills for fish as to it, and were quite sure it was that woman that had taken its luck from it with her 'bad eye.' Many a time after that we had to try to keep things out of her sight, and it was not easy; she would be up and out as early as ourselves, no matter how early we would be. I have seen us up at four in the morning, and even at two, trying to get the salmon boxed before she would get her eyes on them."

We must add one other protective formula from the neighbourhood of Ardrishaig. "This," said the reciter, "is a good protection against injury by an Evil Eye. I used it always with reference to the young chickens, and found it kept them from being hurt by any greedy person." The words are: "*Beannachd Dhia air do shuil; sop muin mu do chridhe.*" ("The blessing of God on your eye; a splash of urine about your heart.")

The translation is given as received, but a "sop " is a "wisp," "a loose bundle," "a cowardly fellow." Attention has been called to the *iubhar*, and on 171 to the *Fachan.* Compare the darning needle's use and its one eye to the following found among the Wallons of Belgium. "*Li bwegne*, le borgne. Cette singulière appellation s'explique par la ressemblance vague que le gland et ses levres presentent avec un œil et ses paupières. Expression populaire: *sain-ni s'bwegne*, saigner son borgne, c'est-a-dire [Greek: pisser]." [14]

The same significance is applied to the same thing in the same way in Arabic, *El aaouar* (The one-eyed). [15]

[14] "Kruptadia," viii. p. 24.

[15] "The Garden," p. 138. Sheikh Nefzaoui. Paris 1886.

This is "a word to the wise" which cannot here be considered further in detail, but undoubtedly has much to do with the preventative of the Evil Eye mentioned, and further explanation of much before alluded to will be evident to the one who can read between the lines when we mention that *maistir* is in ordinary Gaelic urine, and *maistrich* is a verb, to churn, to shake together.

One other hint. A native of Garmouth on Spey said, "I have often heard people saying that one peacock feather given away to a person is unlucky to the one that gets it, but that more than one is all right. One time Sandy took one to his landlady's little boy. He noticed that the landlady looked displeased, and it soon disappeared. When he was telling me about it, I said, 'Why did you not take two to her?' He replied he would have done so, but he did not want to yield to her *freits* (superstitious fancies)."

Compare this with what immediately precedes it, and notice that the offering of a single eye—a single feather—of the bird in question carried with it an evil influence.

INDEX

Acallam na Senorach

Acquaintances, divided into two classes

Admiration, expressions of, to be avoided

Albumen

Alum

Amhairc, droch

Animal

An t-olc

Antiseptic

Augury

Bad e'e

eye

One, held by the

Bardic Irish stories

Bawbees

Beannachadh

Dia

Beliefs

Bhioball

Bhuidseachas, sgil mu

Biblical account

Bitten

Black Art

pokes

thorn, sloe

Bless

Blessed

Father

for the purpose of keeping away the Evil Eye

Blessing seems merely preventative

Blight

by the Evil Eye

Blinked

Bodach granda

Bonnet, darning needle stuck in a

Bothan

Bottle

Bridge

Bruchag

Buidseach

dh' oibrich am

Henderson

Hendry

Buidseachas

Burning stick

waved over it

Burnt, if any man's work shall be

Burrach

Butter not to be seen by anybody

Cac eun

Cailb, Samon, Sinand

Cailleach

Cairbre

Caorain dearg

Cap under her two knees

"Carmina Gadelica,"

Cat cure

Ceapag caise

Chaoran, slat de'n

Charm

Charm, operated a

Charmed string

Charms

Chickens*air an cronachadh*

Cholic

Chratachan

Christian dogma

Chronachadh, air a

injury by

Churn

horse nail tied to the

nailing the shoe of a colt to the

scalding the

staff

Churning

spoiled by the Evil Eye

Cinder

Circle formed by the thread

Circular motion

Clach-na-sùil

Cloth thrown over the churn

Clothing, burning a piece of the

Cluais

Coat, wrong side out

Coins

or brooch

three, seem to be the essential number

Columba

Cook protects ducklings

Cormac's Glossary

Corp creadha

Covetous

desire

glance

Cow's head and horns

Cron

meaning of

Cronachadh

air a

air an

air do shuil

cases of

cure in cases of

fhuair mi

is just envy

is quite common

is still in it

Crown piece

Curative

ritual

water

Cure

view to its

Cured by magic

thread

Darning needle

Decalogue

Deide

Deity

Dh'itheas

Diagnosis

Dish struck on the bottom three times

Divinity

Dosgach

Drawing the tether

Droch sgeul

Drovers

looked on with suspicion

Druids, affinity to smiths

Ear, nicking the

Eibhleag as an teine

Eolas

a' chronachaidh

applied for

deide

gach ni'n aite fein

greim

his father had

is from father to daughter

made the

makin'

man

nathrach

performance

practitioner of

professor of

professors of

sul

was kept in the family

woman

Eructation connected with the Evil Eye and witchcraft

Evil Eye

action of an

anybody may have the

avoiding suspicion of

belief in

belief that he himself had an

believed in

believer in the

case of the

cases of the

casting the

cattle more liable to damage from the

churning spoiled by the

counteracting the

cows dying from effect, of the

developed by relation of sexes

different from witchcraft

difficulty of evolving a theory

distinction between possessing an, and doing harm with it

doubts as to the existence of an

effects of the

eggs injured by the

fowls affected by the

having the

horses liable to be affected by the

hurt by the

indirect advantage to those credited with the

is involuntary

is not always involuntary

literary evidence of the

locality of belief in the

modes of expressing the

no visible benefit to possessor

origin of

or witchcraft

people who possess the, may suffer loss

possession of the, ascribed to females oftener than to males

possessors of the, disliked

possessors of the, to be charged to their face

possessors of the, unlucky to meet

reputation of an

scientists

serpent's stone, a cure for the

stirks more rarely affected than cows by the

survival of belief in

symptoms

their

to be referred to active covetousness

to cure the

to keep away the

water

women, believers in the, more than men

young more liable to the influence of the

Eye

diabolical

envious

had struck

has fallen upon her

my

put his, in her

shall not spare

Facail

airson eolas

ceart

Fachan

Farmad na sul

Father, Son, and Holy Ghost

Fhear mhosach

Fiam

Fios

Fios-achd

Fiosrachadh, or *eolas*

Foal

Folklorists

Formula

Galar's easlainnte

Garbh sgeith

Gearr fheidh

Geas-arachd

Germicide the

Ghonadh, air a

mo

Ghuidhe i ris an fhear mhosach

Gisreag

Glance, envious

Gold, silver, and copper

cure

ring and silver coin

or earring

Gonadh

Green lint

Greim

Ground, must not touch the

emptied it on the

Harm

Heifer

Hendry, witch

Holy Ghost

Honeysuckle

Horse collar

repeating its name three times

shoe in the churn

front o't

to sprinkle the water over the

Humming

a symptom of the Evil Eye

Hurtful eye

Hurting and healing, united in one person

Iadh-shlait

Ill-will

Incantation

form of

processes

repeats an

Injured

by *cronachadh*

by Evil Eye

the cow

Injury, protection against

Iubhar

Ivy

Juniper wood

Kicking

Knife

Knowledge

of healing

the result of inquiry

to cause injury

Laochain

Laogh

Lint

Lips

Living and the dead were wont to pass

Look, a foal hurt by a mere

a horse hurt by a mere

cows hurt by a mere

Look, his would *cronach* it

milk hurt by a mere

Loup

Lucky

Magic eye

fluid

mirror

thread

Maistir

Maistirich

Malevolent

Manure

Marriage ring, a sixpence, and a penny

Medicine bag

Meise de mhin

Melted lead

Metal

Milk

a drink of, given to any one suspected of the Evil Eye

deterioration of

taking a mouthful of

Miscall

Mislook

Mordant

Motive

Muin

Mulach an teine

Nathrach

leigheas airson lot

Neck

bare

Neonain, Bun 'us Barr

Neutralise any bad influence

Nicking the ear

Nos Origines

Obair

Oidche Bhealtuinn

Olc

Operator

Overt act

Paid

Pail, half-crown piece in the

Paper, put salt on a

Pay, they do nothing without

Payment, he did not want

Pee, the milk has gone along with the

Perform his charms by means of a bridle

Performance

Peter, Paul, Mary

Piseach

Pisearachd

Piseog

Pisreag

Pokes, three wee

Practice

Practitioner of *eolas*

qualified

unlicensed

Practitioners vary

Praised, animals she had, died

butter scattered by being

hen taken in dead by being

pig injured by being

Preventative

charms

Professional

Professor

of *eolas*

Prognostications

Protection of the Deity

Quern

Quey

Quey*air a cronachadh*

blind

calves

Rag, burn a

Remedy

Request

Rhyme

Rift

Roin

Rowan

Sack of Da Derga's Hostel

Saint Bridget

Salainn, dorlach

Salmon

Salt, a preservative

and urine, sprinkled with

used as a cure and preventative

Sell, risky to refuse to

Serpent's stone

Seven small stones

Sgeith

Sgil mu'n chronachaidh

Sheirbhis, pris airson a

Sheumais Eoin's Pheadair

Ruaidh

Shilling

Shuil, an droch

bhuail an droch

Fluich do

ghabh an droch

mo

thuit an droch

Sign of the Cross

that it was the Evil Eye

Silver brooch

coin

cure

gold and copper

piece

Silver, white

Sixpence to give her

Skill

Skilled

Skin

Slime

Smiths

Snaithnean

Snathainn cronachaidh

dearg

Snuim

Son of Mary

Sop

Sorcery

Spells

Spilling

Spirit of health and healing

Spit

Spitting into the healing water

Spot from which three parishes could be seen

Sprinkle, used regularly to

Sprinkled

Sreang a' chronachaidh

Stanes, bunch o' sea-shore

Stirk

Stone, water dashed against

Stones, and silver, performance with

certain, used for curing in Evil Eye cases

in the pokes

taken from a particular burn

Suil sanntach

Tar, an Islay application against the Evil Eye

T-aibhisdear

Tether, waving it three times over the horse

Teum

Thread, cure

different colours used

green

must always be green lint

red

three knots on the

to be put three times round the child's neck

woollen

Threads, two, one black, and one white

Three articles

Tiomnadh nuadh

Tobar, ris an taobh deas

o'n taobh deas

Toothache, curing of

Toradh

bring back the

meaning of

power of taking away

Transmission of *eolas*

Tre tsuilib na sochaiae

Trinity

Turf, square of

Ubag

Udder

Uisge a' chronachaidh

bonn airgeid air a chuir ann am bowl

dhoirteadh air an t-airgiod

fior

Uncanny ways

Urine as a preventative

sprinkling

stale

strong

Usual proviso

Uvula, fallen

Vet is no use

Veterinary surgeon

Vomit

Water

absolutely putrid

and copper coin, and a darning needle

and stones

and two threads

as a diagnostic of *cronachadh*

bottle of

from a march over which the living and the dead pass

from where the living and the dead pass

must be poured on silver

of silver

poured on three silver coins

sprinkled on the child's face

Whisky

Wish

Witch

Witch, burning

cure

doctor

Hendry

of Endor

reputed

Witchcraft

Witchery

and the Evil Eye

protecting against

resorted to as a cure

white

Wizard, a strong

may have the Evil Eye

red

Wooden bicker

Word, a, must not be spoken

Words

good

Yarn, ball of

different colours of

red

three ply

Yawn

Yawning, an effect of the Evil Eye